Dreams of Idlewood

Book Two

Idlewood Series

By M.L. Bullock

Dedication

This book is dedicated to Victoria Danielle,
a true Southern belle.

ONCE AMID THE ROSES

Once amid the roses bright,
Ruby-red, honey-sweet,
You and I, in laughing weather,
Sang a lay of love together;
Petals falling on our feet.
When shall summer be so light?
Never more!
Oh, never more!

Once beside the snow-drops, drear,
Waxen pale, wintry cold,
Grief and I, in wailing weather,
Sang a dirge of tears together;
Raindrops dripping on the mould.
When shall winter be so drear?
Never more!
Ah, never more!

Jane Dixon
1883

Prologue – Michael

Mobile, Alabama
1873

Michael didn't need the black enamel walking stick with the silver wolf head, but he carried it just the same. A young man of only seventeen, he was very conscious of his appearance. He detested being called the "young master of Idlewood" or the young anything. He considered himself an "old soul"; an old soul who had the misfortune of experiencing youth. Besides dressing like a gentleman and carrying his father's walking stick, he'd grown a beard and mustache. Some of the local gentry still sneered at him, but they would learn to show respect, eventually. Yet for all Michael's attention to the smallest of details, from the placement of the buttons on his jacket to the precise length of his trousers, he still struggled with feeling like an impostor. (He would never be the oldest.) But he worked diligently at hiding such a ridiculous notion from his family and the local gentry, for he was truly lord of all at Idlewood.

Father was dead. The thought brought a small smile to his face. How his death had shocked the old man! Fortunately he died before he could berate his son for killing him so inauspiciously. Michael declared himself to be his heir and, with Percy missing, so he was. Michael had changed his own destiny by the sheer force of his will. He wasn't going to let anything deter his trajectory now—his star rose high. No, nothing would stop him.

Especially not his drunk of a brother.

Percy had never been much of a man. He read poetry to his sisters, obeyed his father's every word, even to the extent of marrying Aubrey, a woman he had not chosen for himself. Percy doted on Tallulah in life and mourned over her in death as if she had been his wife and not his twin. Michael often suspected something incestuous between them, but he'd never witnessed anything provocative or untoward. The truth was Percy and Tallulah were probably the only two people in the house capable of loving anyone, but they'd loved only one another. Michael had been fond of his youngest sister, Trinket, but she had been perpetually frightened of him and yet he'd never harmed her. She was the only one he missed. The only one he cared for in the slightest. He felt somewhat relieved by her disappearance. Love made one weak.

Here he was again, rescuing Percy from yet another embarrassing situation. But it wasn't an act of love or kindness on Michael's part. No, he had other reasons for coming to pull his brother out of another bottle of whiskey.

Fortunately, the owner of the barn where Percy had been found half-naked and unconscious was an acquaintance of the family. For a few coins, the man would keep quiet and the Fergusons could avoid any further scandal. With Tallulah's suicide and Trinket's disappearance, Michael considered that a plus. If only he had no siblings whatsoever. Then he could tend to his mother and Aubrey as he pleased without the need for keeping up appearances. Mother angered him with her refusal to say anything evil against Percy, even when he had shamed the Ferguson name to such an amazing degree.

And Aubrey? She deserved to be punished for choosing to marry the drunkard. She'd chosen poorly.

The carriage came to a slow stop, and Edward LaGrange, his right-hand man and associate, scurried out. Edward was a self-made man, and Michael admired him although his mother detested the sight of him. They were more like brothers than he and Percy had ever been. Both were equally determined to make a name for themselves and come up in the world, and both had been second sons. Michael and Edward wouldn't hesitate to do whatever was necessary to reach their goals. In fact, they'd made pledges to do so, both with the Creel Society and with one another.

In a few minutes Edward returned with Percy in tow. Michael noticed with amusement that his brother's clothing had been soaked through, likely from a pail of water tossed to awaken him from his stupor. Percy struggled to get into the carriage, but neither Edward nor Michael assisted him. Finally he slogged inside and the carriage door closed behind him. The drinking had cost Percy his handsome looks. He was thin now, thinner than even Bridget, who took to fasting far too frequently. Percy's once shiny, golden hair appeared dirty and long, very much in need of a haircut. His clothing was unkempt, he'd lost his jacket and he smelled as if he had not bathed in a week. The odor of stale whiskey permeated his unwashed skin, and the air hung heavily with it. To show his disapproval and perhaps to embarrass Percy further, Michael pressed a handkerchief to his nose. The handkerchief belonged to Aubrey. Percy did indeed spy the monogram but said nothing about it. In fact, no one spoke as the carriage rolled along and slowed some fifteen minutes later.

Michael glanced at the ginger-headed Edward as he departed the carriage, then gave Percy a smirk. "Brother, if you want to kill yourself, there are far easier ways to do it. Why embarrass our family, embarrass our mother and sister, with this unseemly behavior? Not to mention Aubrey. But why do I bother? It is all over now." Through red eyes Percy squinted at Michael but offered no explanation. Typical Percy. He was accountable to no one and loved no one, except Tallulah. The sound of a boat whistle surprised him, and the vacant look on his face faded. Suspicion appeared.

"Where are we?"

Michael leaned forward on his walking stick, his black coat draped neatly behind him over the leather jumper seat. "The time has come for this to end, brother. Tonight you leave Mobile. You may go anywhere you like—Atlanta, Jacksonville, even Scotland if you wish—but you will not return to Idlewood."

Percy wiped his face with a shaky hand. "What are you talking about?"

"It's time to pay. Time to pay for the bad things you've done."

His brother swallowed and with a hoarse voice asked, "What bad things? Are you going to kill me, Michael?"

His brother laughed at him. "Oh, that would be too easy. And that's what you want, isn't it? And you know what I speak of. It was a long time ago, but blood doesn't wash away that easily." Percy didn't argue and Michael continued, "I have taken the necessary steps to cut you off, as they say. In fact, you aren't to use the Ferguson name again. From now on, you will go by Mother's maiden name, Sinclair. There, doesn't that sound suitable, Percy Sinclair? It's all done. Legally, I mean. Since you want death so badly, you are now officially dead. Dead to all of us."

"What have you to gain, Michael? You have it all now!"

"As I said, it is time to pay."

Percy's eyes filled with tears. "I had no choice. I had to protect her."

"Tallulah is dead now and beyond your protection. In the end, your sin meant nothing. It bought nothing. It saved no one."

"Take me home, Michael. No more games."

"Oh, this is no game." Michael inched toward him, leaning deeply on the stick. In the moonlight, the wolf head flashed and gave an evil glint. "Don't make a scene. Edward has gone now to secure your passage aboard the ship. When he returns you will leave my presence. Forever." He tossed a leather packet beside him at Percy. With clumsy fingers Percy untied the leather string and pulled out a document and a stack of money.

"What is all this?" He blinked in the dark. The coach lamp flickered.

"It is a legal document disallowing you any future funding, except for this one-time dispersal of cash. I think you'll find it more than generous."

"A dispersal? Have you lost your mind? Take me home, Michael."

"Pay attention. Time is short now. You are disinherited, Percy. As I said, you are dead to us all. Including Aubrey." Michael couldn't help but smile. He hadn't intended to bait his brother on this point, but he couldn't resist.

Percy's face whitened and he licked his dry lips as he stared at the bundle of bills. "You can't do that. I am a grown man and our father is dead. You have no authority to disinherit Bridget or me. Mother would never allow this."

That made Michael smile. Yes, now was the moment he'd been waiting for. The moment he could reveal to his brother his long-awaited plans. "Yes, yes I can. You see, Mother has seen the light. She agrees with me. You are a disgrace. She blames you for what happened to Tallulah. There are even rumors that Trinket was stolen for ransom because of your gambling debts."

"That's preposterous! I have never gambled in my life!"

Michael continued as if Percy had never spoken, as if he were dead and gone already. "And Mr. Quigley gathered all the testimonies he needed to satisfy the district judge. Judge Calhoun was shocked. How did he describe you? Ah, yes, 'an unscrupulous rabble-rouser.' You abandoned your family, abandoned your wife. Abandonment is a crime, sir. I have been appointed the official Ferguson heir now." Footsteps crunched in the leaves as Edward approached the carriage but didn't enter. Michael had no doubt that he was smiling in the dark. It was good to see the Second Brothers of the Creel Society claim what was theirs tonight!

"Quigley would never betray me, and Mother would not agree to this. What have you done to her?"

"No worry for Aubrey, then? Ah, well. Poor girl. Now get out of my carriage."

"What? I am not going anywhere, brother."

Michael's anger flared, and with sudden ferocity he whacked his brother across the arm and shoulder with the wooden stick. Percy groaned and slumped to the floor. He whimpered and clutched his arm as he stared up at Michael with hurt, fearful eyes.

Ah, yes, I will always remember this moment.

Unwilling to wait any longer, Edward opened the carriage door and snickered at the sight of Percy lying at Michael's feet. Without a glance upward, Michael leaned down, his dark eyes narrowed with a serious expression. In a flat voice he said, "If you return to Mobile, I will kill you. Don't think I won't know. I have friends everywhere, Mr. Sinclair. If you contact anyone at Idlewood, I will kill you. If you ever show your face again, I will kill you. Get out of my carriage. This is your last warning, Mr. Sinclair."

Looking defeated, Percy stumbled out of the carriage. Edward's leather-clad hand closed the carriage door behind him, and no other words were spoken. As the carriage pulled away, Michael tossed the flurry of currency out the window. He didn't give Percy another look. He leaned against his walking stick to calm himself. Edward narrowed his eyes and grunted. "You know he'll come back. You're just putting off the inevitable. It would have been wiser to kill him. Tidier."

"Yes, I know."

"I don't understand."

"I didn't think you would."

Edward grunted again and leaned back in the seat. "Are you insinuating that you are smarter than me?"

"It's no insinuation. I am. But let's not fall out over that small point. I think it is time to celebrate. What say you, Edward LaGrange? Are you in the mood to indulge yourself?"

Edward's face flushed with excitement. In a quieter voice he said, "You know who it is that I want, Mr. Ferguson. There's only one indulgence that will please me."

Michael sat back easily now, his back slumped a little. The confrontation with Percy had exhausted him, and that surprised him. He suddenly had no desire to celebrate, beyond a few glasses of sherry, but he had to keep his right-hand man happy. And if what Edward wanted was in his power to give, why not? Besides, a union between the Ferguson and LaGrange families would please the Creel Society to no end. No doubt his mother would strongly protest such an "unsavory union," but who would listen to the ravings of a hysterical woman?

"And she shall be yours, my friend. In the fullness of time, she shall be yours."

With a grin Edward shook his hand awkwardly. For the rest of the journey the men remained quiet, staring out their open windows into the dank Alabama night.

They'd both gotten what they wanted.

At last. Michael had everything he wanted.

Chapter One—Carrie Jo

"Detra Ann Devecheaux, you owe me big time for this," I griped to the blond beauty while I pulled at the off-the-shoulder ruffle of my ridiculously fluffy blue dress. I'd tripped over the hem of the hoop skirt twice, and I hadn't even left the room yet. I prayed to God that I would survive the trip down the spiral staircase. Detra Ann's solution to my current wardrobe malfunction was to tighten up the silk ribbons at the waist, so now I couldn't breathe either. At this point, I was pretty sure she was trying to kill me.

Rachel looked equally unhappy, and who could blame her? Of the three of us, she had the ugliest ensemble...and that was saying something. Her bodice fabric was a dingy floral print with yellow-orange and brown flowers paired with a dull, mustard yellow skirt sporting an oversize bow that drooped from the front of the hem like a sad pet. At least I was just a big pile of blue satin ruffles.

Detra Ann sparkled, as always, in her raspberry pink dress. It was a hoop skirt like ours, but it didn't have the extraneous embellishments ours had. And somehow, she made it look beautiful. Her gown had a simple cut with a modest bosom and a smooth wide skirt. I suspected that my outfit and Rachel's weren't merely luck of the draw, but then we weren't all the same size. That's what I told myself anyway. No way would my close friend purposefully lace me up in this joke of a dress.

Naturally graceful, Detra Ann moved liked she was born to wear three-tiered petticoats. Her perfectly arranged coils dangled down her back elegantly while my naturally curly hair puffed out from my antique ivory barrettes like two big cotton balls thanks to the Mobile humidity. It was fall, so wasn't it supposed to be cooler now? Why hadn't I thought of wearing an updo? It was too late now, though. I didn't have time to make that kind of change-up. Half of the Historical Society was waiting for us downstairs in Idlewood's front parlor.

"Are you sure these outfits are historically accurate, Detra Ann? They're pretty horrible. Except Carrie Jo's. I wish I'd picked blue," Rachel pouted, her dark eyes disapproving of what she saw in the mirror.

I laughed. It was either that or cry, and my eyes were watery enough. For the past few days my nose had been running like a faucet. I believed it was from the changing of seasons, the pollen or something. *Perhaps I'm just allergic to this dress.* I took a daytime allergy pill to offset the mucus and hoped it kicked in soon. "Please, girl. I look like a hydrangea bush, and the three of us look like a trio of over-the-hill Azalea Trail Maids." Well, we weren't that old, but I wanted to distract Rachel from her unhappy mood. It didn't work.

"And what color would you call this skirt? Dijon mustard?" Rachel frowned into the mirror as she blasted a few random wisps of dark hair with hairspray. "I'm convinced someone robbed an old couch to make it."

"I think you two look lovely." We both paused fussing over our final touches to shoot her synchronized dirty looks. She relented with a sigh. "Okay, I agree, Rachel. That *is* a god-awful dress, but you are beautiful no matter what you wear. And Angus is going to love it! He is going to meet you at the garconniere. That's where you'll tour tonight. Keep to the script and you'll do fine."

Rachel paused and stared at Detra Ann from the mirror. "Wait. Angus is here?"

"Yes. Was I wrong to invite him? I thought you two were, you know, getting cozy. And we needed a man to play the part of the bachelor. I mean, what's an old bachelor pad without a bachelor in it?" Detra Ann pretended not to notice Rachel's irritability. My assistant seemed on edge lately, despite the progress we'd been making on the house. It had been six months since we'd uncovered the truth about Tallulah and Trinket, and we had since quietly laid their bodies to rest together on holy ground.

With nothing else to distract us we'd worked our magic on the front parlor, the conservatory and the aforementioned garconniere. The antebellum bachelor digs were only about fifty feet from the house, but it was nearly windowless and had an odd tower like the kind you'd see in a castle. It seemed an odd feature, and one could argue it was a forbidding place, but so far I had not experienced anything negative in there. Rachel was much more sensitive to things than I was, though. Most of the time I only dreamed about the dead; she could actually sense them. And from the get-go, it was clear she was not too thrilled about this idea. During our planning meeting she'd muttered something about the outfits being triggers for spirits, but she refused to talk more about it. She'd been out of sorts ever since we began working on the idea, and with my own stuff going on, I couldn't bring myself to pry. Besides, if she wanted me to know, she'd tell me. She knew I had an open-door policy. Especially for her.

Yes, Rachel was a sensitive. She often felt things before they were ever seen, smelled or dreamed about.

She plopped in the gilded cushioned chair and said, "Okay, I'm just putting it out there, but I'm not comfortable going to the garconniere. There is a presence in there, and not a very nice one. I've seen this thing a few times, both in the house and in the tower. It, he, well, whatever *it* is is evil." She shivered thinking about it. "And to make matters worse, whenever Angus is around, it shows up. Almost every single time! It's like this Shadow Man has it out for him, or Angus attracts it for some reason."

Still sounding perky, but obviously disappointed, Detra Ann wore a small frown as she shuffled through her file keeper and pulled out a few papers. "I wish you had told me that earlier." She took a deep breath and handed a sheet to Rachel. "But I came prepared. Use this script, and how about you and Angus take the parlor? Henri and I will hold our presentation in the bachelor's quarters. Can either of you play the piano? We thought that would be a nice touch."

Rachel scanned the paper and gave one of those long, exasperated sighs, like a teenager. "Heck no, unless it's a CD player or a karaoke machine. Oh, wait! Angus can play the guitar! Is that okay?"

"Um, no. I don't think this is the guitar crowd." To me, Detra Ann said, "There is some sheet music on the piano; tell Ashland to use it. He took piano lessons in middle school." To Rachel she said, "No guitars for this, I'm afraid."

"Just as well. I doubt he has it with him. So CJ and Ashland take the conservatory, and we take the parlor? What am I supposed to do in there? Hand out cigars? Read poetry?"

"Yes to all of that. You know what the goal is, sell our restoration services to the community. I know this seems crazy, but trust me, it will put Cotton City Restoration on the map! There's no time to teach you the script, but use it as a guide. Serve drinks, regale them with some stories about the house. Talk about some of the processes you've used in restoring the parlor, point out the features. But most importantly, sell them on the idea of preserving Old Mobile. That's what I had planned to do. You know enough about Idlewood to keep them intrigued. Stay focused on the goal. We want to sell our services but behave as professionals." I could see Rachel's unspoken comment: *In these dresses?* Thankfully she kept her mouth shut because Detra Ann was a hair away from breaking down in tears. I knew her well enough to know she hated surprises. At least in business.

"And let's keep Desmond Taylor happy. No ghost stories or mentions of this Shadow Man. Let's put on happy faces and do this! Those people down there want to invest in Mobile. Let's save the old houses! We can do this, y'all!"

Through watery, itchy eyes I smiled at her. You could take the girl out of the cheerleading squad, but you couldn't take the cheerleading out of the girl. Or something like that.

Gee, my head feels fuzzy. Please tell me I didn't take the wrong allergy pill. That's all I need, to pass out in front of a pool of potential clients.

If I was a drinking woman, I'd have had a few nips to keep me going before making the long stroll down the staircase and into the conservatory. Whose bright idea was it to dress up like this anyway? We were a professional restoration company now. Did we really need a gimmicky stunt like this? I sighed, stood up and tried to tamp down my ruffles. "Well, you're the PR expert, Detra Ann. We're all in your hands."

"Then trust me. This kind of stuff works."

We walked down the long staircase one at a time. Each of us paused on the steps below, stacked behind one another for our photos. Yep, Detra Ann had even sprung for a professional photographer. I prayed to God that I wouldn't end up on the front page of the Mobile Press Register this weekend. Our "menfolk" were waiting for us at the bottom of the stairs. Naturally, Ashland looked like he'd stepped right out of the past, handsome and "put together perfectly" as the old-time Southerners used to say. He wore a light brown morning suit, with a white collar and blue cravat. He'd been talking with some of the visitors until they noticed us take to the stairs.

Someone whistled, and I blushed even though I was sure it was for Detra Ann. But it was Angus whistling at Rachel, and despite her earlier misgivings about her dress, she was beaming from ear to ear now. He offered her his hand as she took the last step. I breathed a sigh of relief that I hadn't tripped during our processional. "Carrie Jo, you look lovely," Ashland said with a smile. The watching crowd politely clapped at our arrival. I blushed or flushed; I couldn't tell which because I thought I was running a fever now.

"Thanks," I said through a stuffy nose.

Of all of us, Angus was the one who looked the most historically accurate, as if he'd stepped out of the past. His massive red beard made him look like an authentic 19th-century gentleman in his black suit with white collars and cuffs. He looked so authentic that it gave me goose bumps. After making some introductions, the visitors were divided up and Ashland and I led our group of about thirty men and women into the conservatory.

"What? I thought we were in the parlor," he whispered like a freight train.

"Change of plans." I smiled at him and squeezed his hand.

The sun would be going down soon, and the large windows of the conservatory gave us a brilliant view of the gardens and the garconniere beyond. There weren't too many color-ful flowers this time of year, but the hedges were skillfully sculpted into spirals and there were other points of interest to enjoy too. You couldn't see Idlewood's sunken gardens from here, but they had not yet been fully restored so that was probably for the best. I was very excited about the pro-spect of bringing that unique space to life. I hoped to find someone competent enough to recapture its beauty.

Each couple was supposed to lead a group through the house, making stops along the way to show the improve-ments we had made. Through the thirty-minute presenta-tion, we'd have a chance to build relationships, exchange ideas. But since Rachel's last-minute confession, I guessed we'd all stay in one place now. That was a shame because I loved the parlor, but as Detra Ann reminded us, this was about our future together. She'd sold the antiques store and kept the apartment above, but I didn't see her and Henri staying there forever. They'd sunk their nest egg into Cot-ton City Restoration, and we had invested the proceeds of the sale of another one of Ashland's properties. Even Ra-chel was a part owner of the business. I hoped we could make it work. So far, so good.

"Why don't you begin, Carrie Jo?"

"Be ready to hit the keys when I give you the cue."

"What? You have to be kidding me. I can't play!"

"Detra Ann says you can, and if you object you can take it up with her."

He rubbed his forehead, and I wagged a finger at him. "Don't even think about it. You know I can't sing, or play or dance. It's you or nothing."

"Fine, but you'll regret that decision. I'll hang out in the back and play when you're ready." He glanced nervously at the sheet music, and I patted his arm.

"You've got this, hon. I've never heard you play, and I'm looking forward to it."

"You shouldn't," he said, frowning as he turned the page.

Oh goodness. That sure didn't sound too promising. "Good evening, ladies and gentlemen. Since our time is limited, I want to begin our presentation now. Please have a seat; I think we have enough seating for everyone. If not, we can find more." The group chattered as they took seats on the settees, couches and folding chairs. There was an eclectic mix of visitors at tonight's event. Some were real estate folks, some were heirs to old homes, others were just curious investors who'd heard about the success we had with Seven Sisters and now Idlewood. I'd scanned the finalized guest list last week, and I was pretty impressed with some of the names I saw there. "Good. Everyone comfortable?"

I walked to the windows and began my speech. Unlike my stressed-out assistant, I knew every part of the script since I wrote most of it. I knew what to feature in this room: the windows, the oversize fireplace and the ceiling medallions. I tried not to think about how close I stood to where Tallulah's casket had rested. I didn't think about Percy's broken heart or Dot's sad eyes. I blinked my eyes, ignoring their sluggish, sticky feeling. *Yep, that allergy pill was kicking in for sure now. Get it together, CJ.*

"You guys are the luckiest group of visitors here today because you get to experience the conservatory at the right time. When we move to other parts of the property, the light will have changed and it will be too dark to appreciate the wonderful landscaping just outside these windows. Just think what it must have been like to end the day here, the sounds of the piano tinkling in the background. As you can see, we've taken great pains to reproduce the gardens as precisely as possible, just as they were when they were first built."

A tall man in the back said, "You mean, what you *think* they looked like, right? Or do you have access to sketches of the original garden? I mean, without them you couldn't possibly know what the original landscape looked like." I didn't recognize him, but he seemed vaguely familiar, like I'd talked to him before. Maybe I had.

"I'm sorry. I don't see a nametag. What's your name again?"

"My name is Austin Simmons. And yours?"

"Oh, excuse me. I should have led with that, right? My name is Carrie Jo Stuart, and this is my husband, Ashland Stuart."

"You owned Seven Sisters at one time, didn't you? I can't imagine why you would give that house up. It's a glorious building with an interesting history." Ashland stirred beside me but said nothing. I could tell he didn't like the guy. Simmons had a nice-looking face and expensive clothes, but he didn't seem to have any manners because he kept talking and cutting into my presentation time. "It has good bones, as they say. Has this restoration been as exciting to you?" *That's a weird question.*

"Well, thank you for your questions, Mr. Simmons. We worked hard on the restoration of Seven Sisters, just as we're happy to work with Mr. Taylor here at Idlewood. It's kind of become our life's work, restoring Old Mobile. As far as comparing the two, that's a bit unfair. This house isn't quite as old, and the layout and features are different. But I think it is crucial—and I know Ashland would agree with me—absolutely crucial that we don't allow these old homes to disappear." People whispered to one another, and from what I could hear, it sounded like they mostly agreed. As the sunlight began to fade, Ashland walked to the light switch and turned the dial so the chandeliers shone their low amber lights.

Simmons didn't get the hint. "Tell me, Mrs. Stuart. Is it true what they say about Seven Sisters? Is the place haunted?"

I laughed nervously and thanked my lucky stars that Desmond Taylor had not made it into our group yet. Mr. Taylor was gracious enough to allow us to use this place for our presentation, for a discount on his final bill, of course, but I knew for a fact he wouldn't like to hear such comments or comparisons. He was a staunch unbeliever in the supernatural.

"Mr. Simmons, if you'll hold off on those questions, I'll be happy to answer them privately after the presentation. All right?" With an amiable nod he sat back in his chair with his arms crossed and watched me, a small smile on his face. "Now, everyone, you may have noticed that the house is positioned so the sunset could be on full display here. That was not a coincidence but smart planning! You see at the time this house was built, and up until the first part of the twentieth century, these grand old homes were built to be appreciated all day long. For example, many homes had 'morning rooms' like the parlor you'll see in just a bit. That's where the family would begin their day, sometimes even taking dinner there and using the dining room only in the evening. As the sun moved across the sky, the residents would move about the house; they began the day in the morning room for optimal light and then in the afternoons moved into rooms with adjacent doors so they could enjoy any breeze that might be flowing. In the evenings, they would come to the conservatory to watch the sunset or step out just beyond to the balcony to enjoy a drink on the patio that oversees the sunken gardens. The people who built Idlewood knew what they were doing."

I felt Austin Simmons' eyes bearing into me as I continued my comments. Yes, that allergy pill was kicking in now. My skin was flushed, and I wanted nothing more than to take a nap. I moved to the oversize fireplace and began highlighting the carved details, the expensive stonework and the reproduction process. I described the ways we'd repurposed a similar mantelpiece for an upstairs room and answered a few polite questions. Mr. Simmons kept his mouth closed but watched everyone who spoke like a hawk. I felt as if he knew all about me. Could he possibly know I was a dream catcher? *No, that's crazy talk.* I felt tired, and my mouth was dry after fifteen minutes of talking nonstop. After a few more minutes I wrapped up the presentation, explaining how we could help the gathering with their own restoration processes. "As you know, we work hand in hand with the Historical Society during these operations and in many cases are successful in adding buildings to their register. That's crucial if you want to qualify for grants and additional funds from the state. It's not as complicated as you might think. And I think that's it for now. Ashland?" I nodded at him, and my face felt sweaty. "Now for a bit of fun, my husband will play for us. We had a piano brought in especially for the occasion." Ashland's face said it all. He didn't want to do this, but he was too polite to refuse Detra Ann or me. I suddenly felt sorry for him, but there was no helping him. The crowd of potential customers and Historical Society members clapped politely as he sat down at the piano. Well, he looked the part of a country gentleman if nothing else.

After a few rough starts, he'd made it through the first page, but there was absolutely no doubt—my husband was the master of many things, but the piano wasn't one of them. Before I knew it, Austin Simmons was standing beside us. "Obviously someone brought you the wrong sheet music, Mr. Stuart. If you wouldn't mind, I think I know this. It's Chopin's Raindrops, isn't it?"

With a suspicious frown, Ashland slid off the piano bench. "I am surprised you could tell. Please, be my guest." We took seats near the front as Mr. Simmons played Chopin like someone who knew what he was doing. In fact, he sounded like some kind of virtuoso. I glanced around the room and saw most everyone was enraptured by his performance. I studied him as he tapped on the keys with his long fingers. *Where had I seen him before?* He had dark, wavy hair that he wore slightly long, but that was purposeful, not in an unkempt style. He was as tall as Ashland, maybe slightly thinner. As he played he closed his eyes, as if he were willing the music into being. I felt Ashland glance at me, but I didn't dare look at him. I was blushing or flushing again, and I didn't want him to misinterpret the effect. I wasn't attracted to the man; I had a fever. Or something. I felt my bosom redden and as if he read my mind, Simmons caught my eye. At the last notes, the applause began and I couldn't help but join in. That's when I noticed Detra Ann and her group had joined us. I walked over to her and she whispered, "Who is that?"

"Someone from the group. He offered to play for us. Austin Simmons is his name."

As our group rose I directed everyone to Detra Ann, who decided now would be a good time to go check on Rachel. "I'm worried about her. And you too. Your face is red, girl. Are you sure you are okay?"

"I think I have a fever, but I'll live."

"Good. Well, send Ashland to the garconniere. Henri is charming, but he doesn't know much about the history of the building or the restoration process. I'll step out to the parlor and check on Rachel and Angus. They should be sending their folks this way soon."

My head was swimming; it was all too complicated. I whispered to Ashland what she wanted, and he left looking relieved. Except for the distrustful glance cast in Mr. Simmons' direction. At least no one would ask him to play again.

Drinking a few sips from my water bottle, I patted my warm cheeks with a few splashes of water and went in for round two. To my surprise, Simmons was waiting for me. "Mr. Simmons, your group is in the parlor now. Just down the hall there." I smiled through my hazy vision.

"If you don't mind, I'll stay with you. I like hearing you speak."

I blushed, I think. Yes, he was familiar. Or was it a fever? "Have we met before?"

"I can't say for sure. Do you think we have?"

"Do you always answer questions with questions, Mr. Simmons?"

It was his turn to blush now. "I would like it if you called me Austin. And forgive me. It is a bad habit I picked up over the years. I would like to stay, though. You have such a passion for this house. I hear it in your voice; it is refreshing."

"I think you'll find that everyone here loves these forgotten Mobile properties, but it's up to you, sir." Unsure what to say, I walked away, my pile of ruffles making a distinct sound as I tried to move as elegantly as possible. It wasn't as easy as one might think. I began my presentation all over again. Sometime during my tour of the room, Simmons disappeared. And that disturbed me too. I was even more convinced that I knew the man from somewhere.

I didn't know what that meant, but I was sure it wasn't anything good. I managed to get through the rest of the half hour without passing out. By the time it was over, I was ready to ditch the itchy clothes and hit the hay. Baby Boy was under Momma's supervision tonight, and I welcomed the undisturbed sleep. I dozed off as Ashland drove home and vaguely remembered us climbing the steps to our room. Ashland wanted to talk about Simmons, but I didn't have the energy to put two words together, much less argue about the strange man.

As I snuggled into bed, it finally occurred to me where I'd seen Simmons before. He was the spitting image of David Garrett! Before I could stew over the strange coincidence, for surely that was what it was, a warm glow surrounded me.

The glow that accompanies a dream…

Chapter Two—Aubrey

Bridget found me in the conservatory, and as usual her hair was disheveled and her gown not completely cinched. She had the wild-eyed look of someone who could see what others could not. In her own way, Bridget was a pretty girl, but not so obviously fair as Tallulah had been. She would never be a great beauty, but she had a vulnerability that some men liked, including Edward LaGrange. Like it or not, she'd caught his eye and, as he was Michael's closest friend, she would marry him. Of that there was no doubt. Michael would not abide disobedience.

I had just finished my practice session; my back and fingers ached, but Michael insisted that I spend the time necessary to perfect my piano performance. Our engagement party was tomorrow night, and he expected nothing less than perfection. I'd returned to Idlewood only this week, I'd temporarily moved back home to Cherry Hill at Michael's request. He wanted to protect my reputation, he said, and would not tolerate gossip about me or him or the Ferguson family. It was bad enough that Percy had shamed me with his heartless abandonment, he said. And since the legal matters were not settled at that time because of his uncertain whereabouts, I had no one to provide care for me. In this my father eagerly accepted my brother-in-law's offer of a monthly stipend. I did not know the amount, but apparently it had been a generous one. Cherry Hill was now filled with new furniture and even gas lighting. We were the talk of the town.

For quite some time I secretly hoped Percy would return to me and to his family, but after six months I gave up hope. He might have been willing to abandon me, he might have suspected the truth about what I'd done, but he would never have abandoned his mother and youngest sister unless something prevented his return. That I fully believed. I read every newspaper I could find, visited the local jail once a month, and the asylum, and the hospital as often as I could. No one had laid eyes on Percy Ferguson, and Michael eventually managed to have him declared dead. I tried to talk him out of it, but he would not be dissuaded and even appeared offended by my intercession on his brother's behalf.

In my heart I couldn't believe that my beautiful husband had died, but how could I prove otherwise? Now here I was returned to Idlewood, a place of unhappy memories and shadows and spirits. A place where my past crimes dogged my steps and oil paintings of dead Fergusons watched my every move. They knew who I was and what I had done. I felt my soul shrinking every time I traveled the hall of the upstairs gallery. The portraits of Percy and Tallulah haunted me, especially their eyes—so alike they were. Their images convicted me from their lofty places.

After a year of mourning for Percy, I was told to put my black clothing aside and prepare to take on the Ferguson name for the second time. My father did not ask my thoughts on the matter, and I did not make a fuss. What would be the use? There would be no society wedding, just a quiet ceremony at the Ferguson Chapel on the grounds of Idlewood. I could not even invite my dearest and oldest friend, Laurel Bennett.

Now Bridget fell into my lap and sobbed. With desperate eyes she gazed up into my face. "Please, sister. You have to help me! You know I cannot marry him. I don't want to marry anyone." Bridget clung to me, her bony fingers digging into my arm. I could feel the desperation in her voice, and her skinny body shook with fear, but what could I do? I had no control over my own destiny, much less hers.

Any thought I had of encouraging rebellion was quickly quashed as Michael appeared over her shoulder. He watched me, his dark penetrating eyes boring into my soul. I had to get this right. "Oh no, Bridget. It is God's service to be a wife." I licked my dry lips and swallowed the horrible lump in my throat as I lied to her. "You get used to it, my sister. Trust me in this. We will prepare the most beautiful wedding gown and trousseau. Perhaps you will travel for your honeymoon." I smiled at her and hugged her, avoiding those empty eyes.

I whispered into her ear as I held her, "Don't fight him, or it will go worse for you." I spoke the truth. Although Michael and I had not spent much time alone together, he frightened me. He wielded the quiet power of a madman; even his own mother feared his anger. It was not an uncontrolled anger, not like a child's. It was like fuel for his tempestuous soul, and it was the secret of his power. Unlike some men I had observed, mostly my father's acquaintances, Michael's anger did not confuse him. It had the opposite effect. It brought him clarity and did not cloud his mind. I did not love him, for he was not my Percy. He would not be gentle, and never would he love me. I was something to be owned, bartered and used when necessary.

Just like Bridget was at this very moment.

She crumpled under my words, then pushed me so hard I nearly fell off my bench. With the speed of a thin whirlwind, she whipped away and left me alone in the conservatory with her brother. She moved too fast for me to call her back. Bridget had always been a strange bird. "And how is your mother today, Michael? I have not seen her come down all day."

"Alas, poor Mother. She was too weak to leave her room this morning, but I am sure she would welcome a visit from you." I doubted that very much. Mrs. Ferguson did not approve of me or of my impending marriage to Michael, and she was not silent on the matter. I was surprised Michael allowed someone to speak so openly against him. As I carefully folded the sheet music and placed it on the top of the piano, my hands shook, revealing my perpetual nervous state. "Since you have finished your practice Aubrey, come with me. There is something we need to discuss."

"Very well," I said as I walked behind him. I followed him to the second floor and into his private rooms. I had peeked inside once, but that had been while I was still happily married to Percy. (If you could describe our marriage as happy. I had been, certainly.) It was a dark room—the darkest in the house, possibly because it was in the southwestern corner—but I noticed that heavy, dark curtains hung in here.

"Please come in." I swatted a fly that buzzed around me and did as he asked. He closed the door behind me. This felt wrong, I couldn't understand why he wanted me to come here. All of his dealings with me had been proper until this point. He'd never so much as kissed me or held my hand longer than a few seconds. Now I worried that he had something illicit in mind. This after all my brave talk to Bridget.

Oh, Percy! How am I ever going to allow him to touch me?

I glanced around the room—even the furniture was dark; only a few lamps burned low. It was certainly a man's room. There were no flowers, no woman's touch, not even a picture. It was austere, sparse and much cooler than my small but sunny room. Michael sat in a padded wooden chair, but he did not invite me to join him. I waited to see what would happen. What could he want to discuss?

He had a silver coin on the table, which he played with as he eyed me curiously. "Do I make you nervous, Aubrey?"

"I am not sure what to say, Michael." He rose from his chair, a stiff smile on his face. Finally I asked, "What is it you want?"

"I want you to look at me like you looked at Percy." He touched my hair, whispered my name in my ear and then circled me as if he were inspecting a piece of furniture that he might like to purchase. "You aren't the most beautiful woman in the county, or even the brightest, but it is you that I want. Tell me why that is, Aubrey."

Angered by his appraisal of me and before I could think properly, the words slipped out of my mouth. "Because I was your brother's wife. I think you want all things that belonged to him. I see his footstool there. And his hunting rifle. Am I to be added to this collection?"

He stopped his pacing, but I did not venture to look at his face. Michael sat down again; his hands rested on his knees now, and his piercing gaze sank my soul. "At least you understand me. More than some. I would not want you to enter into a marriage with me thinking that I loved you; that I worshiped you or adored you. Not that Percy did either. The only person he ever loved beyond himself was Tallulah. I think you are the reason she hanged herself from that tree. Don't you?"

I stared at him and stammered, "I...I don't know. How can I know?" I spotted the glint of his silver-topped walking stick nearby. I swallowed and remembered the first time I had witnessed his use of it. It had been last year when a visitor to Idlewood made an offhand comment about Michael's horse. He'd snatched him down and beaten him bloody while the rest of the Ferguson family watched. I'd begged Percy to do something, but he'd left the mess behind, taking me with him. I'd not seen such an evil outburst since, but that was enough to frighten me into submission. Even the servants whispered in fear when Michael's dark anger threatened to emerge from within him.

Rubbing his mustache thoughtfully, he unabashedly stared at my breasts. "I want to see what I am purchasing. Remove your dress."

"What?" I asked stupidly, my face flushing with embarrassment at the thought.

"Remove the dress. I want to see your body. Just to settle my mind. I need to know that I will be fully satisfied with whatever you have hiding under there."

"I am not a horse or an animal to be purchased. If you are to marry me, why would you shame me in this way?" I whispered, red-faced.

Michael reached for the walking stick and slammed it once on the table. "I am not accustomed to disobedience, Aubrey. Do as I ask." With fumbling fingers I complied. I untied my ribbon and let the skirt fall to the floor, hoping that would be enough. I covered my most intimate area with my hands, but he would not be denied.

"More," he said in a low, commanding voice.

"Michael, please," I whispered, but his eyes told me he would not relent. I unlaced the bodice and let the fabric slide off my body. I cupped my breasts with my hands and bowed my head in shame.

He leaned back, and the chair creaked under his weight. After a minute he leaned forward on his walking stick and said in a rough voice, "More." The only thing left between my future husband and me was a thin muslin skirt. I tugged at the knot, refusing to cry. I could not show weakness; men like him reveled in it. How alike he was to my father! Finally the knot released, and I let the skirt fall to the ground. I stepped out of the fabric and refused to look at him. Instead I fixed my gaze on Percy's rifle that hung on the wall. *This is how you survived! You didn't think about the moment!*

Michael walked toward me, staring at various parts of my body like a man looked at a squirrel he was about to dress. *Yes, I'll cut here, here and here.* I shivered at the thought. Without a word he walked out of the room; I could hear his boots thumping down the hallway. I dressed quickly, before he returned. Who knew what he would do next? I had no mirror to rearrange myself in, but I left the room thankful that nothing more severe had happened than the crushing blow to my pride.

If only every night would be like that. I could endure his nasty stares, but his touch—I could not stomach the idea that he would touch me in the most intimate of manners.

Before I retreated to my room to hide in shame, I had to visit Mrs. Ferguson. She didn't care two figs if I visited, but I knew Michael would know whether I had obeyed. And I was an obedient woman.

I tapped on the door, but no one answered. Her personal maid, a shriveled wasp of a woman named Lita, was not lingering by her door as she usually did. Bridget was God knew where. I swung the door back and saw a shadow dart across the room. "Lita? It is Aubrey. May I come in?" No answer came, and I pushed the door open a bit more. I saw it again. A small shadow. My hand froze on the doorframe. "Hello? Mrs. Ferguson? May I come in?" No answer, only the ticking of a clock. It was well past dark now, and there was no light to fight back the invasion of inky blackness. I remembered that Lita usually kept matches and a lamp on the side table. Mrs. Ferguson could not see very well and sometimes needed additional light even on bright days. Leaving the door open, I lit the lamp and carried it to Mrs. Ferguson's bedside. Immediately I could see the woman was dead and in a horrible state. I nearly dropped the lamp when I saw the frightened, frozen look on her face. Her eyes were wide and staring at something horrific. Her mouth was open too. She wore her nightgown and kerchief still, and her hands were folded neatly on the coverlet above her body.

I heard a stirring behind me. Felt the shadow before I saw it. There was something in here with me. I heard the giggling of a familiar voice.

I screamed and didn't stop screaming until Michael found me.

It was true. This was a house of death.

Chapter Three—Carrie Jo

Feeling tired and sunbaked, I collapsed on the hotel bed and laughed at Momma as she did the same. "Whatever calories we ate today, we had to have worked them off. I've never walked so much in my life. Have you?" My feet felt hot and my cheeks were stinging, but it had been a wonderful day.

"Nope," she confessed. "And I've never eaten so much shrimp in my life either. I think it's safe to say I ate like a pig. It's a good thing these shorts have a stretchy waist." As we lay in our beds enjoying the air conditioning, we both sighed happily. This had been a welcome vacation for us both. The first ever, actually. Momma's recovery from her head injury hadn't been as quick as she or any of us would have liked, but at least she remembered who I was now. Until her freak accident I'd never heard of post-traumatic or retrograde amnesia. I kept my fingers crossed that all was well with her now.

We'd had a glorious time strolling the beach boardwalk. Like a pair of excited tourists, we'd cruised the endless rows of artists' booths and naturally came back to the hotel room with ocean-themed knick-knacks, hats and t-shirts. I had seen it all, but we weren't scheduled to return home until tomorrow evening. I resisted the urge to immediately pick up the phone and check on baby AJ. Surely Ashland wasn't feeding him chocolate or doing some other crazy dad thing with our son. But despite my frequent "mommy moments," I was glad I came. This was my first National Shrimp Festival. It was billed as one of the largest festivals in Alabama, and judging by the crowds there was no arguing that. I looked forward to returning next year, hopefully with Ashland.

"What's next on the agenda, Momma? You still want to make the historic homes tour in the morning? It's a lot of walking too. Trust me. But I'm game if you are!"

"Ugh. My feet are going to need more time than that to recover. How about we skip that this time? Let's sleep late and have a nice brunch together. I'd like to check out Hemingway's, the little restaurant in the hotel lobby downstairs."

I flopped back on the pillow and closed my eyes. "That sounds perfect."

She added cautiously, "And…maybe we can chat."

I opened one eye and looked at her. By her tone I could tell *chat* meant talk about us, about our troubled past, and that caught me by surprise. "Okay, Momma. Who gets the shower first?" I wanted to immediately ply her with questions, but I showed some restraint. My mother's therapist encouraged me to be patient, to let her initiate the conversation and take responsibility for what she did. But to say that it was difficult was an understatement.

One thing for sure was that Deidre Jardine had a difficult time talking about any kind of painful memories. And to compound the situation, that freak accident left her with some memory loss. Recently, I'd walked in on her crying more than once, and on another occasion she'd surprised me with a long, desperate hug before walking away again in tears.

Honestly, the change in her was beyond remarkable. Three years ago I would never have dreamed that we'd ever have a happy relationship. She'd never physically harmed me growing up, but the mental abuse—for that's what it had been—left me struggling with trust issues. To this day I had no idea why she decided to finally seek medical help, much less move to Mobile to be near me. Whatever the reason, I was grateful. At first I had been extremely suspicious, even leery about letting her back into my life or near my family, but I'd taken a chance at Ashland's and Detra Ann's encouragement. One last chance. And I hadn't regretted it. My mother was truly a changed person.

"Dibs!" she shouted like a kid. "Boy, one of those big fruity drinks with the pineapple chunks would be good right now. Without the booze, of course."

"You got it! I think I'll call home. Make sure Ash hasn't diapered the baby's head or left him at Small Steps."

"Haha! Give him more credit than that, Carrie Jo. He can handle two days with the baby, and AJ is such a good little boy. He hardly ever fusses."

I laughed in agreement. "I know I'm being ridiculous. But you must know how it is. Detra Ann calls it New Mommy-itis."

With a wistful look and a nod she said, "Yes, I remember."

"I really have enjoyed myself the past few days, Momma. I hope you know that. And look at our tans."

"Me too, kiddo. And as you can see, I don't tan nearly as well as you. I spot and freckle. I'll be out of the shower soon." She slipped off into the bathroom, and I dialed home from the hotel phone.

I waited for it to ring, heard static on the line and then heard muffled voices. What a horrible connection! "Ashland? Is that you?"

The whispering continued, as if I'd connected with multiple lines, like an old-fashioned party line, not just my home number. One voice, a woman's, sounded louder than all the others. I couldn't make out a single word, but her tone was desperate, as if her life were hanging in the balance. Perhaps it was!

"Hello? Is someone there?" Static blasted in my ear, and I hung up the phone, my heart pounding ninety miles per hour. I dialed the number once again, and this time my husband's husky voice poured through the receiver. I breathed a sigh of relief.

"Whoa, kiddo! Hey, babe! You caught us at bath time, and your son thinks he's at Splash Mountain." He sounded amused, and baby AJ's delighted squeals in the background made me miss him all the more. Unlike some children, he loved his bath.

"Um, I just called to see how y'all were doing. The first time I called I had a weird connection. You having problems with the phone?"

"Nope. We've been outside playing in the yard."

On a hunch I lowered my voice and asked, "Anything else going on? Any kind of...activity?"

He got quiet and then said, "Ah. No. All is well here. You sure you aren't just looking for a reason to cut your vacation short? I swear we are both alive and looking forward to our pizza later."

"Pizza?"

"Babe, it was a joke." With a worried tone, he continued, "You having a good time in Gulf Shores?"

I smiled at his ability to see right through whatever façade I tried to slap up. I wasn't good at faking a happy mood. But I was happy, wasn't I? "Let's see. I have a nice sunburn, to be followed by a farmer's tan. I broke a flip-flop. And I ate my weight in shrimp. All in all, I'd say my first trip to the Shrimp Festival was a complete success."

"How about the presentation? Hey, kid—cut that out," he said with a laugh. "Daddy doesn't need a bath right now."

"It was hardly a presentation. Really informal setting, and it wasn't at the convention center like we thought it would be. Last minute-change of plans. I showed the pictures and answered questions. There were more people there than I expected, and I left with a few dozen business cards. Lots of interest. You sure you want to do this? Restoring one old plantation is a lot of work—as you know. Can you imagine doing that nonstop?" That was responsible Carrie Jo speaking now. She was always a party pooper. The truth was I was just as excited as my husband, but I guess I wanted a little assurance, for us both.

"We're doing this together, right?"

"Yep, always together, Ashland. I love you, by the way. Thanks for this time with my mother. It was a nice surprise."

"Oh, I'm full of surprises."

I laughed at that. "Not in front of AJ!" I joked. Then the line went dead again, and a weird clicking sound filled my ear. Before I could hang up and redial, the whispers returned. One voice sounded familiar, but I could not quite identify it. It was as if whoever was speaking was being intentionally vague. Then the line went truly dead. I hung up and picked up the receiver again multiple times, but there was nothing there now. Not even a dial tone. My cell had died earlier and was charging in the car. Maybe now it had enough juice to call home. I turned to find my mother's fearful face staring at me.

"What's wrong? And don't lie to me, Carrie Jo. I can tell something is wrong. Is it the ghosts? What do we do?" She was getting hysterical, and I squeezed her hand comfortingly. Her face paled, despite the ton of sun she'd gotten earlier.

"There's nothing to do. I don't know who it was. It's going to be okay. I promise. Would you like some water? Here—come sit here." I patted a pink pleather chair and dug around our mini fridge for a bottle of water. I found one, cracked it open and sat across from her at the glass-topped rattan table.

"I don't know how you handle it all the time. I never could."

I froze. Did she mean to tell me that? Might as well ask. "You have experience with ghosts, Momma?"

She nodded as she slid the towel from her hair and pressed her hand to her face. "Only in my dreams."

"Why didn't you tell me? I could have—I mean, we could have helped one another."

She took a big swig of water, and we both jumped as the hotel phone rang. With shaking hands I picked it up. "Hello?"

It was Ashland making sure I was okay. I assured him I was, talked to baby AJ and told him good night and promised to see them both tomorrow afternoon. "Take your time, babe. We're going to play ball at Medal of Honor Park tomorrow."

"Have fun! Love you!"

"You too! See you, Mommy."

AJ gave me a raspberry, and I hung up. "How about we order a fruity drink and something light to eat from room service?"

"Yes, let's do that." Then she leaned back with a sigh. "You must hate me—I have been so…unreliable. I left you alone to handle all this, but I didn't know what to do. I still don't. You know more about all this than I do, and you didn't have anyone to guide you. I guess we do need to get it all out in the open. I've put this off for too long already."

I couldn't believe my ears. Was I ready for this? Did I want to know? What if knowing destroyed our relationship? I didn't want to lose what we had now.

She must have noticed my hesitation. She said, "Why don't you take your shower. I'll call our order in."

"All right." I grabbed soft cotton pajama shorts and my favorite Snoopy t-shirt, then went into the bathroom and closed the door behind me.

I could hardly believe it. In a few minutes I'd finally have the answers to my "why" questions. I'd know who my father was, and maybe I'd learn something about Chance Jardine.

It was time to hear it all, wasn't it? I washed the sweat off my body, shampooed my hair and skipped the conditioner. I was anxious to hear what Momma had to say before she changed her mind. Thirty minutes later, we were finishing our dinner (although there were no fruity drinks) and I was feeling even more anxious.

"I don't know where to begin," she said. I slid the plate to the side and waited for her to sort her thoughts out. Neither of us ate much, and I felt the tension between us rising. For a second, I had a mean thought: *Well, I'm not going to help you explain yourself.* But like the therapist said, it was best not to confront her with my own feelings at this stage of the healing process. That made sense to me, and I didn't want to be a conduit for further hurt. Betrayal, bitterness, the vestiges of a childhood with a mother wavering on the edge of a complete mental breakdown. Yep, I had issues.

But the woman who'd done that wasn't the woman who sat across from me now. My mother wasn't that person anymore. And for the life of me, I couldn't figure out how she'd managed to climb out of that deep dark hole of depression. Or whatever it had been. My insides flipped remembering her dreams. She'd climbed in the bed with me once in a while when I was a child, and I could see her dreams. Could she see mine? Her dreams were filled with bare trees, slithering snakes and empty houses. One particularly frightening night, I'd seen her screaming and wrapped in snakes, but there'd been nothing I could do to help her. The vicious things hissed and snapped at me if I tried to reach for her or help her. I'd screamed myself awake and had run away to cry somewhere alone. As a kid, I simultaneously hated her and felt as if I'd let her down.

"If you aren't ready to do this, it's okay," I said sincerely. Yes, there were many questions, and I did have unexplored wells of anger, but if finding answers meant losing her, I didn't want to know. I couldn't lose her again. I'd rather never have answers than lose this relationship my Momma and I had worked to build.

"I can dream walk too, Carrie Jo, but I guess you know that now. That's what my aunt and grandmother used to call it, dream walking."

I whispered it back to her. "Dream walking?"

"I suppose there's a fancier name for it, but my family wasn't very educated, at least not formally. We didn't know what else to call it. Pauline, my grandmother, your great-grandmother called it dream walking, so we all did. And she was the strongest one of us, until you were born. People would come from all over the state to ask her things. If someone went missing, people would show up at the house, begging her to come with them to dream walk their property to find whoever or whatever it was that had been lost or missing. Sometime she would go, sometimes she wouldn't. I never understood how she made those decisions, but she was a woman who kept her own mind about things."

"Do you have pictures of her?"

"No, I'm sorry. I don't. My mother lost everything in the house fire. Including all those old photos. I wish that wasn't the case. You remind me of her in more ways than one."

"Really?"

She nodded and took a sip of her water. "One night, a man came to the house. A big man, I'll never forget how tall he was, probably the tallest man I'd ever seen. I was never allowed to sit in on these requests, but I always spied, like any kid." With a nostalgic half-smile, she continued, "Grandma Pauline left one night and never came back. After that, my mother moved us out of the old house and we traveled around awhile. My father died in the war. I really can't remember him."

"I'm sorry to hear that."

"You don't have to be. You probably hate me for keeping you from your father, but maybe you'll hate me less when you know everything." She covered her mouth with her hand, and I could tell she was on the verge of tears.

I squeezed her hand. "I don't hate you."

She seemed relieved at my answer. "I guess it's time to be honest and let the chips fall where they may. I loved Jude Everett from the first day I met him. He worked at the bookshop around the corner from my house. He was five years older than me. Dating him seemed wild, risky. At least for me. I never strayed too far from the fold as a teenager. Jude and I had some good times together, until we got married. Until I saw his dreams." She sobbed now, and I went and got the box of tissues from the bedside table.

I sat back down, handed her a few tissues and studied her face. "What did you see, Momma?"

"Terrible things. Things I could never tell a living soul. But he never knew I could see him doing those terrible things, not at first. The first time I saw what he did, I thought I was sick, had a fever. I wanted to believe anything but the truth. Anything but that. Then I saw it again. In gory detail. It broke my heart. Still I didn't say anything. I kept quiet until I couldn't anymore. I was so afraid. If you'd seen what I had seen…"

Great. I finally get to hear something about my dad, only to find out he was evil. "That is horrible, I can't imagine what that was like." With her hands on her face she shook her head. I could sense her fear even after all this time. "Well, let's back up a little. Tell me the good stuff first. What did you like about him? You know, when you first met him."

She nodded and blew her nose. "When I first met him Jude was patient and thoughtful; always so helpful when I came into the store. He'd put books back for me. As soon as I walked in he'd say, 'I've got something special for you, Dee.' He was not Casanova handsome, but he was attractive. He had a nice voice too. All that stuff matters when you're seventeen."

"Where was he from? The same town as you? Denton Falls?"

"I don't think so. I never really knew. He told me so many half-truths I couldn't be sure. I'm sorry." Then she snapped her fingers. "But I do have a picture of him. I managed to save a few pictures." She dug in her denim purse and produced a small envelope. There were several photos inside, yellow and curled at the edges.

She handed me one of a man holding a baby.

"Is that me? Is that my father?"

"Yes, that's you and Jude."

I blinked and stared at the face, the very familiar eyes, the curly brown hair. "I have to know what you saw, Momma. I have to know."

"Carrie Jo, you wouldn't thank me for telling you. I can't tell you. Please don't ask me to." Her voice quivered, and I relented.

"Okay, I'm sorry for pushing you. I'm grateful for any information you want to share. Please understand how curious I am. And trust me, I've seen evil. If you change your mind, I can handle it, Momma. Don't you think I should know?"

"No, I don't. I don't think even I should know. I wish I had never met him, and I'm sorry he's your father. I should have done better for you; I should have done better for Chance. But I can't change the past, CJ." She started crying again, and I flinched at hearing Chance's name.

"So he's real? I have a brother? Is he my brother?"

"Oh yes, he is very real, Carrie Jo, and he loved you so much." She handed me another picture. "This one is your brother. Look how alike you are. Same eyes, curly hair. Such pretty babies."

I couldn't believe my eyes. I just blinked at the picture as she continued, "One day I came home from work, and he was gone with your father. Jude had taken you to my mother's, and then he left with Chance. He didn't want us to see what he was doing, Carrie Jo. I could see who he was, who he really was under that sweet smile and quiet manner. We could dream about what he did. And he couldn't have that."

"And what about my brother. What happened to him?"

"I wish I knew. I think about him every day. I let him down. I let him down! I should have left when I saw that first nightmare. What Jude did was evil. I tried to find Chance, I wanted to find him, but I couldn't. I dragged us from town to town following his trail. The police wouldn't help me. They thought I was a nut, even when I described the crime scenes. Then when they found the…evidence, they suspected me. I told them the truth, Carrie Jo, but they wouldn't believe me and I couldn't convince them to. Even my mother turned her back on me. She never liked Jude, and I think she wanted to punish me for disobeying her to be with him. It all sounds so fantastic, even to my own ears."

I studied my father's face again and listened to her words. The sensation was like shockwaves washing over me. "Crime scenes?"

"Please don't ask me anything else. I can't do it, I just can't." She began sobbing again, and I squatted down in front of her and held her.

"Hey. It's okay, Momma. It's going to be okay. We're your family, we love you." I hugged her tight, and she clung to me and wept. I cried too, but I didn't let myself get out of control. She didn't need that. Neither did I. "What do you say we go home? It's only an hour's drive."

"Yes, I would like that. Are you sure you don't mind cutting our trip short?"

"No, I think it's time to go home. It is home now, isn't it?"

"Yes, it is home. Do you regret my coming to find you, Carrie Jo?"

"Never. And Baby Boy loves you. We all do." I hugged her one last time, and then we packed up our souvenirs and suitcases and headed back to Mobile. It was dark out, but I wasn't the least bit tired. I was ready to go home and get started on my search.

I had to find my little brother.

Chapter Four—Rachel

"Angus, I can't do that. It's my job you're talking about. If I got busted being at Idlewood when I shouldn't be, especially as part of a ghost hunting team, I'd get canned." I brushed the hairspray out of my hair, gave him a disapproving look in the hallway mirror and stalked off to the living room. He wasn't far behind. "Correction: It's not just my job, it's my business now. I can't believe you are really asking me to do this."

"What? You said it yourself, you aren't just an employee anymore. Now you're a shareholder. You have every right in the world to be on that property. And you can't say you aren't a little curious, Rachel. You've got ghost hunting skills of your own. You are a sensitive! If we went just for a little while tonight, I'm sure we'd see something after all the activity in the house today. I don't need to call Eric in on this, just you and me."

"You want to creep around Idlewood in the pitch black hoping to find a ghost. You know that place has a presence, and yet you want to go poke it in the eye? Let's compromise. I'll let you poke around tomorrow after work."

"The best time to hunt ghosts is at night."

I flopped on the couch next to him and tossed the television remote in the empty space between us. After a long night of stomping around in a horrid dress and smiling constantly, I was ready to veg out on the couch. But apparently Angus had other plans. I knew it wasn't a great idea to invite him to tonight's event. That's why I didn't! I wished Detra Ann had asked me first. Angus and his buddy Eric were obsessed with ghost hunting the grounds at Idlewood, and I was obsessed with Angus. Did he feel the same way about me? I seriously doubted it now. I mean, here I was, here he was. We were in the house by ourselves. I even tidied up my bedroom before I took off tonight, you know, just in case we met up afterwards, but he didn't seem to care or even make the tiniest move on me. And how had he kept his invite to Idlewood a secret?

"That was a one-time deal. Trinket is at rest, and I want it to stay that way. She doesn't deserve a bunch of folks stomping around her grave. Besides, how can we be sure that wasn't just a fluke? I haven't seen much of anything since then, except that thing. I want to keep it that way."

"But how can you be sure? And what about the Shadow Man? Are you going to tell me that he's at rest?"

I frowned at him. "I don't think it's a ghost, and I sure as hell do not want to communicate with it. Why is this so important to you? It's not like Idlewood is the only haunted house in Mobile. Why the fixation? And I want you to tell me the truth. No more BS, Angus."

He unbuttoned his dress shirt to reveal a blue t-shirt underneath. Angus had nice arms; he looked like he worked out, but I knew he didn't. He was just naturally fit looking. He pulled off the shirt, and I tried not to stare. He tossed off the last vestiges of tonight's outfit and laid it on the cushion next to him. If he thought I was feeling sexy now, he was sadly mistaken. "What makes you think I'm not telling you the truth?" Those blue eyes said *trust me*, but I didn't. He was holding back, I was sure of it now.

"I may not be a human lie detector like Detra Ann Devecheaux, but I can smell bull crap a mile away. My father was the biggest BS'er who ever lived; you are small potatoes compared to him. Now give it up or get out. I'm done being used, Angus." *Gee, where did that come from?* Apparently I was plenty ticked off at him. Well, I had a right to be. At least Chip had the courtesy to show up with a bottle of wine now and then. And Gran liked him even though she called him "Big Ears" when his back was turned. Angus and I'd been "dating" or whatever you call it for six months now, and we'd barely kissed. So far, I wasn't getting any of the things a young woman was supposed to be getting from her boyfriend, physically or emotionally, and I was pretty pissed off about it.

"When have I lied to you?" His innocent-looking expression did not move me. I frowned at him, and he sighed. "You're right, I didn't tell you everything, but I didn't want you to think I was crazy." I leaned back and crossed my arms across my chest as if to say, *Okay, spill it.*

"I've had some experiences of my own at Idlewood. That thing, the Shadow Man, he touched me, and I haven't been able to forget it. It was a long time ago, but I'll never be the same until I understand why it happened and why he won't leave me alone. I have to have answers. You don't know what it's like. The anxiety, the overwhelming fear. Just when I think I've escaped him, he finds me."

Then it hit me. I knew exactly who he was. How could I have been so blind? "You're Beatrice Overton's son. The one who lived at the house when the crib incident occurred. I read about that online."

He didn't deny it and seemed excited that I knew something about it. "Yes! That was me. I have to know that what I saw was real, Rachel. It almost drove my mother crazy.

She talked about it until she died." *Big whoop. We've all got a sad story.*

"So from the day we met until today you used me. You used me to get in the house." I was growing more agitated by the second.

"No! That's not true." He ran his hand through his red hair and frowned at me like I was the one in the wrong. Like I'd been holding back on him. "I didn't know you were working there, but when I met you, it was like a ray of sunshine. A sweet surprise. I like you so much, Rachel. I wanted to tell you about all this, but I was afraid you would think I was just some nut job."

"And now I think you're just a jerk. I want you to go, Angus." His shocked expression didn't move me. "Take your innocent look and your beard and your accent and get out. I don't like being played for a fool. Or used. And that's what you did, no matter how you want to pretty it up." I was so mad I could cry. In fact, I felt a fat tear slide down my face. I wiped it away furiously. "I want you to leave." He hesitated for a moment, then grabbed his shirt and walked out the door. I slumped back on the couch as I heard the front door close.

"That didn't go so well. What were you thinking?"

"Gran! You scared the crap out of me. How long have you been standing there?"

She crunched on an apple and leaned against the doorframe, staring at me disapprovingly. "Long enough to know that you made a total ass of yourself."

"Gran!" I didn't even think she knew that word, let alone used it. "What's the matter with you? You don't even like Angus! What was that you told me? 'He's going to get you in trouble.'"

"Oh, I remember what I said. But we're past that now. You love him, and he needs you. He needs your help. That thing is following him around, and he can't get rid of it on his own. Eventually, it might even kill him."

"How can you know that?"

She sat in the plaid rocking recliner next to me and put her apple core in the tiny trash can she kept next to her chair. "Think about it. Every time you see that thing, your boy-friend is around."

How does she know that? "He's not my boyfriend, Gran."

"You are missing the point, Rachel-girl. Think for a minute and stop letting your pride get in the way."

"I'm not—it's a matter of trust. You understand that, sure-ly." Even as I said it, I began running through the incidents in my mind. "Do you think somehow the Shadow—"

"Stop saying its name. It knows its name, what we call it, and it likes to hear it. It makes it stronger. And yes, I do think somehow they are connected, but not on purpose. I mean, he didn't invite it in, not like that. But I think that thing is his familiar. Maybe something his mother dabbled in that he didn't know about."

"But I thought familiar spirits were friendly?"

She laughed suddenly and shook her head. With a cautious eye around the room, she hopped up, walked to the mantelpiece and lit a row of dusty, pale yellow candles. She'd had those candles for years and had never lit them before. I watched silently, my nerves pricked up, and waited for her to finish whatever it was she was doing.

"Honey, it's been my experience that those kinds of entities are rarely friendly. They have a mind of their own and their own agendas. I've heard there are rare exceptions, but I think it boils down to classes of spirits. There are ghosts of the dead, troublemakers in life and afterwards, then there are the ghosts that need help. But these other entities, like the one we are talking about now, well, they are something altogether different. Strong, evil energy, concentrated, fixated on one thing or one person. Set on its destruction."

"That makes sense, but trying to purposefully communicate with these things, that's not something I'd want to do."

"Who does? But if you can see them and they can see you, what choice do you have? You have to learn to deal with that world and keep it in proper prospective."

"What if I don't want to deal with it? What if I want to go back to being a normal person?"

She chuckled at my answer. "Normal? When was any Kowalski normal? I'm not, you're not. As my mother told me, 'Embrace the weirdness and be yourself.'" All of a sudden, Gran's parakeet blasted a sharp, shrill sound, and I practically jumped off the couch.

"Good Lord, that bird almost gave me a heart attack!"

"Animals are sensitives too."

I laughed nervously and watched the candles flicker. Suddenly the front door opened, and Gran and I gasped as we heard footsteps in the foyer. I heard keys jangling and a sound like a purse being set down on the table. I breathed a sigh of relief as I realized my mom was home from work.

"I think I need a drink," Gran announced as she leaned back against the couch cushion. "We're in here!"

My mom's head appeared in the wide doorway of our front room. "Hey! What's for dinner? I'm starving. I'm lucky I got out of there before this storm rolled in. It's lightning over the bay; I think we're in for a real doozy." Her smile disappeared when she noticed the candles on the mantelpiece. "Mom, Rachel? What's going on?"

"Rachel's boyfriend is being stalked by a spirit, but it's not a ghost."

Mom walked into the living room and flopped in the recliner. "Oh dear. What are you going to do?"

Gran whispered to Mom as if I couldn't hear her, "Rachel's mad that he didn't tell her about this 'thing' sooner."

"Gran, please stop acting like I'm not here; like I'm a kid. I can hear you, you know."

"Then do what's right."

"Wait a minute, Mom. What's going on here?"

I rolled my eyes, feeling aggravated. "Gran, I thought you were concerned about my welfare, all worried about me because of the house and the spirits. Now you want me to go engage this thing on behalf of a guy who has played games with me for six months? I don't understand you."

"He makes you happy, and he's a fellow human, and I'm willing to help you. If we can help him, we should. It's the right thing to do. But of course it is up to you, dear. If you feel he's done you so wrong that you can't forgive him, as a woman I respect that. However, as your grandmother and someone who knows about these spiritual things, I hope you will reconsider. You need to learn how to use your sensitivities in a safe way."

"Mom, if she's not ready, you can't force her to engage that world. And I am sure that whatever force guides Angus' life will find a way to lead him out of danger. There's no need to put Rachel in danger too."

"Bree, you know as well as I do that if she doesn't use her gift she'll lose it! Rachel, just ask your mother. One day you'll wake up and have no sensitivity at all. Isn't that right?"

"Yes, that's right, but I have no regrets. I don't feel guilty about it. I gave it up for a reason, and that's my choice. Just like Rachel has to make her own choice about this. I love you, and you have been good to us, but I don't want you to pressure her."

Gran let out a rough breath and her shoulders sagged. "I know, I know. I guess I'm just a nosy old lady."

"Mom, I never said that."

Gran rose from the couch and headed to the kitchen. "Whatever you decide, then. You are probably right. Well, I better get supper going. How does breakfast for dinner sound?"

Mom spun her ponytail and made it into a bun. She leaned back in the chair with a deep sigh. "How are you, Rachel? I meant what I said. It's up to you. She means well, but it doesn't mean you have to do what she suggests."

"I'm so confused. It's not that I'm all that afraid, except for Angus. And he lied to me."

"Did he?"

I looked at her like she was crazy. "Well, yeah."

"If that's the best he can come up with, then you'll do okay." Then in true Mom form, she changed the subject. "Ugh! My dogs are barking. Hey Mom, maybe we should order a pizza."

"Yuck," she called back, "I'll have dinner ready soon. What about you, Rachel? You want a couple of eggs and some bacon?"

I slid my feet back in my shoes and reached for my keys off the coffee table. "No, I'm not really hungry. I think I'll go for a drive."

"Want Gran to save you some?" I tried not to look too deeply into my mother's worried eyes. I'd just made a big deal about being a grown-up. I couldn't crawl up in her lap now.

"Yuck. Cold eggs and greasy bacon? No thanks. I'm not that hungry. See y'all later." I headed to the front door and reached for my crossbody purse. When I left I had every intention of heading to my thinking spot, the swings at the park, but that's not where I ended up.

When I finally put the car in park, I was sitting in the driveway of Idlewood.

Chapter Five—Carrie Jo

Momma and I didn't talk on the way home. It wasn't an uncomfortable silence; we both had things to think about. Like what could my father have done that was so terrible? I'd personally witnessed a number of crimes as a dream catcher, each horrible and hard to forget. I couldn't imagine what she must be feeling. To see someone you love act like a monster. But he was a monster, wasn't he?

And to think my little brother was out there somewhere. Maybe. Who knew? God, that would be awful. I stole a glance at her as she stared out into the darkness. I felt bad that I could be a source of discomfort for her, but I was grateful to finally know the truth—or some part of it. With a hug and a promise to call tomorrow, I dropped her off at her apartment and made the trip the rest of the way home as quickly as possible. It was quiet this early Sunday morning. Not much traffic, and I didn't bother to turn on the radio. The low hum of my vehicle kept me company. That and my thoughts. Yes, it was too quiet. I left my bags in the car, grabbed my purse and let myself in the back door of Our Little Home. Thankfully, Ashland had not locked the deadbolt, but I did. You could never have too much protection.

I found my husband snoring in the big chair in the living room; Baby Boy was cuddled up in his arms. Ashland held our son like he was a football that he had to protect from all opponents. I smiled at the sweet sight. The baby's blond hair was moist, and it stuck to his sweet face in a kind of half halo. I loved napping with him. He was so happy, his dreams were happy. I didn't need to hear the words; I knew he loved us and knew he was loved.

What about Chance? Does he know that somebody loves him?

"No, Carrie Jo. Not tonight. This is life, your life. Enjoy it," I warned myself. I touched the baby's forehead just to make sure he didn't have a fever. Nope. He was perfectly fine. My son sweated like crazy when he slept, no matter what time of the year it was. As quietly as possible I eased him out of Ash's arms. I should have known he would wake up. Lately he slept pretty lightly. My husband opened his sleepy blue eyes. "Hey, babe. What are you doing here? What time is it?"

"It's late—or early. Close to one, I think. We decided to come home early. Surprise." I kissed his cheek and then the baby's.

"Everything okay with you and Deidre?" He rubbed the sleep out of his eye and stood, stretching his back.

"Let me put AJ down, and I'll meet you upstairs. Unless you'd rather sleep alone here in the recliner."

"No way." He grinned up at me like a lazy cat. "And I'd rather not sleep at all."

I smiled at him as I climbed the steps. Baby AJ didn't make a sound or even stir. I turned on his baby monitor and softly closed his door. Funny how most nights I prayed he'd sleep all night. Tonight I kind of wished he'd wake up and smile at me. Did he think I'd abandoned him? But I wanted to spend time with Ashland too. I had so much to tell him, but right now I didn't want to tell him anything. Except that I loved him and needed him.

Ash met me at the door of the bedroom with a long, sexy kiss. His skin felt warm, and I got caught up in the appealing combination of soap and designer cologne. Goodness, he smelled so good! We struggled with clothing for all of fifteen seconds and spent the next little while being Carrie Jo and Ashland. We got lost in paradise, as he liked to describe it sometimes. Then he fell asleep again and I cuddled up to him, happy that I'd come home. Tomorrow I would begin my search. I would help my mother find Chance. We just had to bring our family together. At last.

It felt like I'd just closed my eyes when they were open again. But I wasn't Carrie Jo anymore. I whispered her name. And then I was her. I was Aubrey.

***

My hands patted the wall beside me. It was cold and slick. I did not like the feel of it, but I had to find a way out of this place. I forced myself to calm my breathing. If I wasn't careful I would make myself sick again. It wouldn't do me any good to faint now. The creatures hiding in the dark would gnaw on my flesh and I'd be dead! I knew they were there because once in a while I could hear them moving, scratching, clawing.

Oh God, help me!

It was no use; he didn't help sinners like me. I'd been calling out for help for hours it seemed, and nobody had come to my rescue. A small animal scurried past me, and I screamed again as its nails clicked on something nearby. It sounded metallic.

"Somebody! Help me!" I yelled again. My cries bounced back in my face. Besides an angry squeak, the sound of my voice was my only answer. Feeling desperate, I fell on all fours and crawled around in the dark. Perhaps I could find a lamp or at the very least a weapon to shield myself from the rats. Suddenly I bumped my head on something. I rubbed my forehead and felt no blood. I put my hands out in front of me and let my fingers explore. It was wood—a wooden beam! It was a relief to touch something besides stone. So I was not locked in the mausoleum! I gasped in relief. All my life I'd feared being buried alive; it was the one fear I never told anyone.

I reached up and felt around in the blackness. Not a beam—yes, a board! I pulled myself up carefully and traced it. I almost vomited when greasy fur rubbed against my arm as the rat fled past me. He'd leaped down from somewhere above. What if there were more? I refused to let go of the board. If I did I felt sure that I would never find it again. My hair had fallen in my face, I was sweating profusely now and my clothes stank like wine and mud. Yes, I remembered now. I'd been at a party! With Michael.

I felt another board, and another, and another. This was a ladder! I climbed it until I bumped my head again. I was underground for sure, but where? Why couldn't I remember? I searched for a handle but felt nothing. Banging on the wood with my fist, I screamed louder, "Please! Someone, help me! I'm down here!"

No one came to rescue me. At least an hour went by, but I refused to move from my spot. I had to believe I would get out. I wrapped my arm around the beam and waited. Waited for the rats, death or whoever locked me in. Beneath me I heard the rat running about again, angry that I'd invaded his space and disrupted his solitary plundering. I wanted to weep, but I was so thirsty now that I wasn't sure I could cry. Perching carefully on the ladder I banged on the board above me with all the strength I could muster. If only I wasn't a wretched sinner! Then I could pray to God above to rescue me. But no way was I worthy of any rescue. I was a murderess. A liar. And that was just the beginning of the list of sins that weighed on my soul. If it hadn't been for my letter to Tallulah, she would be alive. And little Trinket...and most certainly my Percy. I could have found another way, but I had been impatient and selfish.

Percy! My husband! My true husband! How I miss you!

I would never see his face again—even in the Gloryland to come. For sure I would be denied the pleasure of his presence. In heaven, all would be revealed. Percy would know my sins, and he would hate me for them. No. It was better to live and avoid his scorn, if possible. Perhaps I would die down here. Certainly there was a purpose for being here. Michael had to have delivered me to this hellish place. He hated me—that I knew for sure. Michael loved no one, not even himself.

What was that? I heard footsteps on the boards above me and the sound of a heavy door opening. I banged on the wooden board above with both fists.

"Please! Let me out of here!" I heard the scraping of wood and saw slender beams of light filtering in now. I could see! I wanted to look around me, assess my position, but my eyes were riveted on the square of wood above me. It had begun to move. Then a thought occurred to me: what if this was Michael? What if he'd come to finish the job? He could easily bury me down here. *No, God! Please!* Instinctively I inched down the ladder, in case I needed to avoid a blow. As the lid opened fully, I blinked against the light, unsure of who my deliverer might be.

"Please, don't hurt me," I whispered as I raised my hands to protect my face. I would beg if I had to! Whatever it took to please Michael. He enjoyed hearing me beg, but I'd done it so regularly lately that I assumed it did not thrill him like it used to. Over the past few months he'd found new ways to degrade me, but that wasn't the worst of it. He forced me to tell him all my secrets. How Percy felt when we first lay together. How often we made love. What sins I had committed. And yes, he knew what sin I committed against Tallulah. Yes, he knew what I had done. He knew my letter almost by heart even though I could not find it. It must have burned after all.

But Michael knew, and it was as if I'd sold my soul to Satan himself.

"No, Michael. Please!" When the expected shower of blows did not come, I lowered my hands and glanced up to see who stood above me. A hand stretched toward me, and I blindly took it, allowing him to pull me up the ladder. When I saw the face of my rescuer, I began sobbing immediately and almost collapsed on the floor.

It wasn't Michael's face I saw. It was Percy! Alive and standing before me! No ghost but living! His beautiful face was no longer golden but pale, his blue eyes no longer sparkling but dull and full of sadness. I suddenly realized how alike he was to Trinket.

"Percy? How can it be you? You are dead, you are dead!" I felt myself falling again, but he caught me.

"We have no time to talk, Aubrey. We have to go! Can you walk?" He looked nervously over his shoulder.

I laughed and cried at the same time. With dirty fingers I touched his face. "Is it really you, my own husband?"

"We must go! Hold on to me." He slung my arm over his shoulder as I stared at him and struggled to walk. How long had I been imprisoned? Surely no more than a few hours. Or days? I was so thirsty!

"Percy, you are dead. I saw you buried! You cannot be here. Am I dead?"

"No, darling. You are not dead. We must run now. To the gate and then into the woods beyond. I know where we can hide."

"Yes, I can run. But don't leave me, Percy. Promise me you will never leave me again. He will punish me if you do."

"I swear it. I won't leave you again. I hear someone coming! We must run, Aubrey! Run with all your might!" And so we did run. I ran with Percy dragging me behind him. My chest burned, my feet hurt in my uncomfortable shoes, and my dark green dress hung off my body like a heavy shroud.

Then I too heard the clanging of a bell, the pounding of horse hooves on the road near us. As the animal approached, we fell to the ground and hid in the tall grasses on the side of the hill. I knew this hill! I'd been imprisoned in the garconniere!

"Now!" Percy whispered, and we ran across the road into the apple orchard. No one followed us, not even the dogs. Eventually they would come. They would find us for sure. But none of that mattered now.

I was with my own dear husband. And we would never part again.

Chapter Six—Rachel

By the time I got out of the car I was freezing. I zipped up my hoodie and made my way to the house. *Okay, spiritual sensitivity, don't let me down now.* I closed my eyes for some reason, as if that would help me zone in on the ghosts of Idlewood. It didn't. I felt nothing and saw nothing for a long time. Finally, I half-sat, half-leaned on the hood of my car and waited, wondering what I should do next.

To be honest, Angus' request didn't surprise me. In fact, I was prepared to go back. I still had my backpack full of the things an amateur ghost hunter might need, including some items I "borrowed" from some of the attic trunks. I found a braid of hair; the ribbon that held it together was marked with Aubrey Ferguson's name. I also found an old cameo and a pair of riding gloves. Yes, I would have gone back if I hadn't busted Angus in a lie; if I believed he wasn't using me for access to the house. But that was then. Here I was now…and of course, I couldn't stop thinking about him.

No doubt I'd acted like a hothead by sending him away like that, and now here I was doing exactly what he wanted, just without him. What was my problem? It wasn't like we hadn't snuck in some ghost hunting before. No, that wasn't it. He'd lied to me, kept a big secret about who he really was from me. That was wrong, a hundred percent. People looked for different things in a potential mate. Some folks wanted to find a playmate, others a soul mate. I just wanted honesty. At least Chip had been honest. He didn't pretend that he liked the supernatural stuff I was into just to get on my good side. And yeah, he could be critical, but he was always honest. That was probably why we dated so long. I wasn't even attracted to him, not like I was with Angus, but that just goes to show. Your body can totally pick the wrong guy.

Yet, I couldn't allow Angus to die at the hands of the Shadow Man. Sure, Gran exaggerated at times, but in this case I'd felt it, knew it was evil. I couldn't imagine that thing stalking me. If there was some way I could get rid of it, or convince it to leave, I would do it. At least try. Even if I never saw Angus again, I would know that I tried.

And still I felt nothing. No trace of a spirit, only the constant sadness, the energy left behind by those who had lived and died on the grounds of this great big house. Idlewood was so different from Seven Sisters. Our first restoration also had an assortment of spirits, but there were times when you could feel that they had loved one another, once. There had been hope there. Idlewood was another matter. Had anyone been happy here? Ever?

The porch light shone bright, and there were a few dim lights shining through the expensive curtains. The second floor and attic had no lights on, and I stared at the house wondering where to start. Then I saw a face, a small, familiar face. Trinket! Why would she be here unless to warn me about something?

"Trinket?" I whispered into the dark, knowing that if it was the girl's spirit, the distance wouldn't make a difference. She would hear me. I didn't see her again for a few minutes, but then I caught a glimpse of her face looking down at me from Tallulah's room. Her hair was long, and she wore her bow tonight. That was weird. Why would she do that? She hated those bows. "Trinket, what is it?" The girl shook her head slowly, just twice, and then disappeared.

Okay, well, Trinket doesn't think this is a good idea either.

A shuffling sound in the nearby azalea bushes pulled my attention away from the upstairs windows. I heard the thud of footsteps as whoever it was quickly walked in the opposite direction. Wait. Could Angus have snuck in here? There was no gate to keep anyone out, as I'd been saying there should be for months. "Hey! Who's over there?" Nobody answered me, but the footsteps moved even faster. They were heavy like a big man's steps, but I still couldn't see anyone. I pushed through the gap in the bushes and walked through the orchard. For a second I saw a fleeting shadow leave the pathway and climb the hill, but he was gone before I could go after him. "Angus? It's me, Rachel!" If not Angus, who could it be?

I began to jog a little now, hoping to catch up with him. It seemed like the faster I moved, the faster he did. I didn't dare take off running—there was more than one gopher hole on this property. Dry leaves crunched beneath my stomping feet, and I zipped the last few inches of my jacket up to my chin. There was a definite chill in the air. Someone close by had burned leaves recently; the musky fragrance lingered in the air. It reminded me of grilled hot dogs and family bonfires from my childhood. My stomach rumbled now, of course. I should have eaten dinner before I left the house. I climbed the hill and despite my familiarity with the Idlewood estate, I was surprised to find that I was now standing in front of the garconniere. Of all the rooms in the house and buildings on the property, I hated this one the most. And that was saying something. I was no fan of one particular room on the second floor. The large window in the front of the looming tower stood open, and it looked like the eye of a giant Cyclops. Whose idea had it been to build this monstrosity? It did not go with the house at all, and Carrie Jo and I had found very little in the way of information about it.

Low, soft-looking shrubs were recently planted around the circular building, but they did nothing to dampen the austerity of the towering edifice. It reminded me of the chess piece—which one was that? The rook? It was just weird. I chewed the inside of my lip, wondering what to do next. The thought of going inside caused stomach somersaults. I'd gotten lucky earlier, getting out of leading the tour out here, but now I was here again. As if Fate or something else wanted me here.

From inside I could hear the scraping of wood, like someone had pulled out a heavy chair in a deliberately jarring manner. Whoever was inside wasn't taking great pains to keep quiet.

"Hey! You aren't supposed to be in there!" I shouted to the closed door. Nobody answered. Surely if Angus were the intruder, he would have said something by now. My senses were tingling and my heart was racing.

"Angus?" I whispered as I tapped on the wooden door. Again, no one answered and I heard nothing. *Big choice now. Do I leave and call someone to come check it out, or do I handle this myself?* Well, this was my big idea, wasn't it? I wanted to talk to this thing. Couldn't back down now.

I tapped again and this time tried the door handle. It didn't budge. Definitely locked. Stupidly, I'd left my keys in the car, and that included the keys to the tower. If I wanted to get in, I'd have to retrieve them. That meant walking through the spooky woods not just once but several times. Did I really want to know who was inside? Stepping over the shrub, I quietly pressed my face against the window. I shielded my view from any glare, but I didn't know why I bothered. It was pitch black inside and almost that dark outside. No lights, not even the light of a clock or a side lamp.

My breath clouded the window a bit now. Yes, it was cold and getting colder by the minute. I peered into the room where I guessed the chair would have been. I saw the chair and indeed, it was no longer under the table. Unless the last person to leave left it out like that. That was possible. Who was the last one here earlier? Ashland? Then I saw it. As dark as it was, the shadow that passed in front of my face was darker. It was no fluke, no trick of the light. It was a figure, like a man's figure, tall and with muscular shoulders and no face. I gasped and nearly fell backwards before I collected my wits and leaned flat against the wall.

Oh no! It knows I'm here! Now what?

The hilltop wasn't that far from me, I could run to it and pray that the Shadow Man didn't follow me. I had never heard of him appearing in the orchard or outdoors at all.

Then the door began to shake as if someone on the inside wanted very much to be on the outside. The old-fashioned metal door knocker began clacking, and the wooden beams of the house heaved under the shifting weight. I began backing away from the house, step by step, my eyes never leaving the doorway. Just a few more steps now and I'd be at the hilltop, then I could run down the hill and through the orchard. I was ready for this. I could do this. The door-knob stopped twisting, the knocker stilled, and the house settled again. I breathed a sigh of relief and waited. I saw nothing, felt nothing, heard nothing.

Until I turned around.

Chapter Seven—Carrie Jo

Sunday morning always arrived early at my house. It was six o'clock, and Baby Boy was letting the world know it was time to get the day started. Thanks to the baby monitor, which seemed exceptionally loud this morning, I could tell AJ wanted to see his Momma right away. I peeked over the blanket at Ashland, who stirred beside me as if to say, "Just five more minutes?"

"I think it is you he wants to see," he said. "Come on, babe. The master of the house has spoken. No sleep for us, and no more lazy days at the beach for you."

I pretended to pout and rolled out of bed ready to see my son's sweet face awake. I paused outside his door to make this moment linger with a game. "Baby Boy...Baby Boy..." I called from the hallway. "Is my Baby Boy awake?" He quieted his chattering to listen, and I said again, "AJ...guess who's here?"

"Momma, Momma, Momma!" I could hear the excitement in his voice, and my heart felt like it was going to burst from happiness. I jumped out from the doorway and he squealed happily. I scooped him up and kissed his face about a dozen times. He giggled and squeezed me back.

"Wow! You partied hard last night, didn't you? Let's get you a fresh shirt and diapers. You ready to go get something to eat?" He raspberried his agreement and grabbed his feet as I hastily placed him on the changing table that was quickly becoming too small for my big ol' boy. He clung to my hip as we went downstairs for breakfast. I smelled the coffee going and was happy to see my husband working on some scrambled eggs. Just at the smell of food our son was practically squalling for his breakfast. Every morning he seemed to forget that we always fed him.

"Ready for coffee?"

"Yes, and make mine a double." I smiled at Ashland between shoveling spoonfuls of baby cereal into our son's greedy mouth. "I know, I know. It's good stuff, isn't it?" I laughed at AJ as he smacked away.

"You got it," Ashland said with a smile. "Now tell me what happened. I thought you were coming home today. Not that I'm complaining or anything. Last night was wonderful."

"Ash! Not in front of the baby," I said playfully. Baby AJ couldn't care less what we were talking about; his little face was scrunched into a plea for more cereal. "I have so much to tell you I barely know where to start. For starters, Momma told me a few things about my father, and I have a picture in my purse." Ashland scooped eggs out of the pan onto two small plates and gave me a look of surprise. "Don't get excited. He's not a nice man. My father, Jude Everett, kidnapped my brother Chance when he was only one, and my mother hasn't seen him in almost twenty years. Naturally she blames herself. I guess any mother would." I swallowed as I watched our son enjoy the last few spoons of his breakfast. I couldn't imagine losing him. What she must have gone through! I sipped some coffee and went back to feeding the baby. My husband didn't rush me, and I shared every bit of information I could remember. He wasn't surprised to hear about my mother's dream catching skills and said as much. By the time the baby was satisfied and I finished the story, my eggs were cold and my coffee cup was empty.

"Well at least you have a name and something to go on now. You are a talented researcher; you'll find your brother."

"How did you know I'd look for him?"

"Because that's what we do, babe, and how could you not? If I had a lost sibling, I would never give up on finding him or her. Family is everything." He squeezed my hand and said, "How is Deidre?"

"She's okay, I think. She got a bit freaked out, though, and that's why we came home. I had trouble connecting with you on the phone; it was like there were voices on there but not yours or mine. She heard it and just kind of lost it. And after her confession, she and I were exhausted. I'll call her in a bit and make sure she's okay. At times like this, I wish she'd stayed with us longer."

"Yeah, but she needs her space just like everyone else. I think being on her own will be good for her." His comment surprised me. Was he giving me a hint about something? Did he need space? I refreshed my coffee while Baby Boy played with what was left of his food. He was thoroughly enjoying himself. At this point he was certainly going to need a bath before he dressed for the day.

While I cleaned up AJ's experimental artwork, the phone rang. Ashland picked up, and I was immediately intrigued by the conversation.

"Hello? Oh, hey, buddy! I haven't heard from you in a while. How have you been? Aw, man...sorry to hear that. You in town? Um, sure. I can meet you for lunch. Where? Just a second..."

I wiped up the remnants of the cereal, which was quickly becoming concrete-like. I tossed the paper towels in the garbage can as my son let me know he was ready to be freed from his high chair prison and go play. "Okay, okay," I said as I eased his chubby butt out of his high chair.

"Babe? Do we have plans today? It's Jeremy. Wants to have lunch with me."

"Uh, no plans that I know of. Go ahead. Me and the kiddo are going to hang out and play in the backyard."

"Hey, Jeremy. Yes, let's meet at Callahan's. Sure, I think there's a game on today. Yeah, I'll see you at noon." He hung up the phone and gave me a big grin. "That's a blast from the past. I haven't spoken to Jeremy in years."

"Wait. You mean Jeremy Stevenson? Libby's brother?" I couldn't hide my disgust. Was Ashland serious? Call me cynical, but was this really a good idea?

"Yeah, but he's nothing like her. Jeremy's had some bad luck, but he's a good guy. You'd like him. Like I said, he's nothing like Libby."

"Well, I hope not."

He laughed, thinking I was joking. With an absent kiss on the top of my head he added, "I'm sure he'd be horrified to know that she behaved like she did. I'm still shocked by it."

"Yeah, me too," I added. I hadn't forgotten Janice Kowalski's warning about Libby. Something weird was going on. My husband and I had been married for a couple of years, and I could not recall him mentioning spending time with Jeremy. Not while we were together anyway. *Okay, Carrie Jo.*

Must you always be suspicious? Let it go and trust him. He has always done the right thing.

"Think I'll sort through my office this morning, maybe tidy up my desk. You guys need anything?"

"Only a diaper change. You game?" I said, frowning at the smelly kid.

"Lucky you. Time to go." He quickly left us, giving me a mischievous grin.

"Perfect timing," I called after him. I watched his big shoulders sway down the hallway. Baby Boy sputtered in my arms, and we headed to change him. "Phew! What's Daddy been feeding you?"

I cleaned up my messy kid and put him in his play gate in the living room when the phone rang again. *Great. I hope it's Libby this time. I'd love to tell her how I feel about her.* I ditched my usual friendly hello. "Yes?"

"Carrie Jo? This is Janice. Is Rachel with you? Y'all working today?"

"Rachel? No I haven't seen her in a couple of days. What's going on, Janice?"

"She didn't come home last night. She had an argument with Angus, went for a ride and never came home."

Worry crept up and down my spine. This wasn't like Rachel at all. She wasn't the kind of girl who just didn't come home. "Are you sure she didn't just get up early and head to Idlewood? Or maybe go make up with him?"

"I'm not sure about anything. I just thought I'd call you first. I guess I am being a worrywart. If you hear from her, please have her call me."

"Sure will. Hey, if you don't hear from her soon, you call me. I'm here if you need me."

"Great, thanks." Janice hung up the phone, and I strolled down to Ashland's office to ask him if he knew anything about this. He wasn't in there. I peeked in on Baby Boy rolling his ball around and clapping his hands, and I smiled as I quickly climbed the stairs. Ash was in the guest room up there. The door was half open, and he was digging through one of the many storage containers that held his hundreds of pictures. He must have found what he was looking for because he sat on the bed and stared at the photograph a good long time. I tapped on the door and pretended I hadn't been spying on him.

"Hey, sorry to interrupt, but have you heard from Rachel?"

"Uh, no, I haven't. Why?"

"Janice Kowalski called and was looking for her. She didn't come home last night."

Ashland grinned. "It sounds to me like Rachel and Angus made up. They probably hooked up and she stayed over. Don't you have his number?"

I sighed with relief. He was probably right about that. "I think so. You think I should call him?"

"Well, no. It's not even eight o'clock yet. Let the girl get a chance to get home before you call and bust her. If Jan hasn't heard from her by this afternoon, then call him." He put the lid back on the storage container and slid it back in the closet.

"Yeah, you are probably right. I should get back downstairs to the kid. You need any help in here?"

"No, I found what I was looking for," he said. And he wasn't anxious to show me what he'd found.

"Great. Have fun cleaning your office." I left him alone and spent the rest of the morning bathing the baby, playing outside in the yard with him and thinking about my family. I wanted to call Momma, but I also wanted to give her space. It was a lovely fall day, warm enough that we didn't need jackets, but I put the baby in a cute blue turtleneck and corduroy pants. He wasn't actually walking yet, but he liked to pull up on things and he absolutely adored the yard. We sat in the grass and played with toys. As he had a good time I let my mind wander. I wondered what Chance had been like as a baby. I was too young to remember our short time together. I wondered if he'd been fussy or quiet. Did he cry all the time? What did he like to eat? What games had we played together? I felt a great sense of loss, but then I reminded myself that there was still a chance I would see him again. Anything was possible.

Baby Boy started to get fussy. He was tired and so was I. I decided to go inside and forage for a healthy lunch since I'd be on my own.

"Babe? I'm taking off. Be home in a couple of hours."

"Enjoy yourself. Say, 'Bye, Daddy!'" I waved the baby's hand while he fussed. Yep, it was almost nap time. My son and I snacked on fruit and he drank his fruit juice before he began rubbing his eyes. Fifteen minutes later, Baby Boy was dozing and I carried him upstairs and put him in his crib. I was just about to call Jan to see if Rachel had come home yet when somebody knocked on the door and startled the heck out of me.

When I peeked through the glass I almost fell on the floor. The face of David Garrett was looking back at me! I sure wasn't expecting that! I stepped back and caught my breath. *Okay, Carrie Jo. Think reasonably.* I peeked again. The face looking back at me belonged to Austin Simmons, not David Garrett. *But how does he know our address?* What if this was work-related? I cracked opened the door and greeted him with a cautious smile. "Mr. Simmons? May I help you?"

"Good afternoon, Mrs. Stuart. I know this is an inconvenience and I am sorry to bother you at home, but I wonder if it is possible to have a moment of your husband's time." What an odd experience, staring into the face of someone from my dreams. Someone I didn't trust. I wasn't sure if I trusted this new incarnation either.

"Ashland had to step out for a minute. Is there something I can help you with? If you have questions about Seven Sisters…"

"It's not that. I'll come back if you like. Will you please give him my card? And it's important that we speak soon. Please?"

"Sure, Mr. Simmons. I'll give him your card." He handed me the card and said with a striking smile, "I do appreciate it. Have a nice day, ma'am." I watched him climb behind the wheel of his silver Mercedes and ease down the driveway. I closed the door behind me and stared at the crisp white card. I read it twice, hardly believing what I read.

Austin Simmons
Ad lucem

I knew it was Latin, but darned if I knew what that meant. A few minutes later I was on my laptop searching the phrase.

"To the light?" I said to myself. "What does that mean?" I then searched for "Austin Simmons" and added "Mobile, Alabama." Nothing. Nada. I took off "Mobile, Alabama" and tried again. There were about a hundred hits, but at first glance I didn't spot his face on any of the social media profiles. I tried the online yellow pages. Nothing there either. I tapped into a few more reliable search engines and came up with zero.

I was beginning to doubt if Austin Simmons even existed.

Chapter Eight—Jan

"Come on, Bree. Let's go to the Stuarts' house. No sense in sitting here and doing nothing—I don't care what the police say. I'm not waiting forty-eight hours to file a missing person report. That's ridiculous!"

"I'm with you, but let me drive." I didn't argue with her. My daughter needed to feel in control of something right now. That was her nature, so practical. Much more practical than I.

"Fine! Whatever, but let's go now."

Sabrina put the car in reverse and headed toward the Stuarts' house on Government Street. I didn't bother to call—a phone call wouldn't have satisfied me anyway. I wanted everyone searching for my granddaughter. I found Angus' phone number on the card Rachel had in her desk, but he swore he hadn't seen her. Naturally my phone call launched a dozen questions from him, and I answered none. I wasn't in the mood to play nice with the boy. I hung up and knew immediately that she was in trouble. That was not an intuition that I shared with Sabrina now.

"Mom, we'll find her. I'm sure she's okay. She has to be okay, right?" Her eyes searched my face for assurance, but I couldn't give it to her. I didn't know what to say. Our Rachel had never done anything like this before, not even during her rebellious stage when she dyed her hair purple and got the Pegasus tattoo she didn't think I knew about.

"Here it is. This is it."

She pulled into the driveway, and I didn't waste any time getting to the front door. Carrie Jo answered right away and immediately knew something was wrong. "No sign of her yet?"

"No. I'm assuming you haven't heard anything either?"

Carrie Jo's son began fussing in the other room. "No. Not a word. Oh goodness, Ashland James is in rare form today. Y'all come inside. I'll call Momma to see if she can watch him for me, and then we'll start looking. Have y'all been to Idlewood yet?"

"No, not yet. I didn't think it would do any good without the keys. She's got her keys with her."

"Okay, give me a sec. Be right back, Baby Boy."

Sabrina and I played with the baby as we waited. He was a sweet child, with a perfectly round face and a playful personality, but I couldn't enjoy the time with him. I was anxious to get the search started.

A few minutes later she returned with a worried look on her face. "My mom is on the way and Ashland is almost home. I'm going to run up and grab my shoes. You guys got him?"

"He's fine." Sabrina sat next to the baby, who immediately started crying for his mother as CJ disappeared up the stairs.

I whispered to Sabrina, "I hope she hurries."

"It's okay, Mom. We'll find her. Rachel is too practical to get in trouble. She's street smart."

I nodded and swallowed the lump in my throat. "You and I both know that's probably where she went." I rubbed my forehead with my hand. "This is my fault. I know it is. I told her to embrace her gift, but I had no idea she would get hurt. I know she's in danger. I can feel it!" I blinked back tears, and Sabrina stared at me.

"Stop that, Mom! Don't talk like that. She probably fell asleep while she was working. You know she's a workaholic. Don't start blaming yourself. What is it you always say? 'Don't borrow trouble'? Now stop." Sabrina's tone surprised the heck out of me, but it was enough to shake me out of beating myself up.

Carrie Jo bounded back down the stairs and sat on the couch next to us while she tied her shoes. She'd pulled her hair back and was wearing jeans and a long-sleeved t-shirt. "Tell me exactly what happened, y'all. When was the last time you heard from her?"

We told her what we knew and by the time we'd finished, Ashland and Deidre had arrived. My mind was totally on Rachel, but Ashland's appearance disturbed me. He wouldn't look me in the eyes, as if he were guilty of something. Major.

"Have the police been notified?"

"Yes, but we were told to wait forty-eight hours. We can't do that."

"Well, I drove by the house on the way here. Her car is there. She's got to be there. I checked around the porch and stuff, but it was locked up tight." When Ashland glanced at me, I could see his blue eyes were worried but not necessarily about Rachel. His face was white, despite his tan. Yes, indeed. Something was amiss with him too.

"Let's go then." I headed toward the door and left them all behind. I didn't give a hoot who came along. My grandbaby needed me! I wasn't a psychic, just a sensitive, but I'd been in tune to my daughter's and granddaughter's energy for years. As I sat in the car waiting for the group to take their cars too, I was so impatient now, too impatient to be my age.

"They'll meet us there. Henri and Detra Ann are coming too."

"The more the merrier, but if Rachel's car is there, she should be there too."

Sabrina focused on driving down Government Street while I offered up a few silent prayers. She was doing a much better job than I would have been. The traffic was too heavy—didn't these people know it was Sunday? A few minutes later we were pulling into the driveway of the big house.

Idlewood's exterior had largely been redone, the old "plaster" concoction of ground oyster shells, pig bristles, lime and sand sloughed off and replaced with some new stucco that was supposed to last for twenty years. It was mold-resistant and could easily be replaced if the occasion called for it. I knew all this because of Rachel. She'd scattered the living room floor with pictures of Idlewood when they first got the job. She knew more about the house than probably everyone in the room right now. That didn't make me like it any better. Even in the bright light of day it reminded me of a great big mausoleum. Nope. I didn't like the place, and I hadn't been quiet about it.

"Oh, Gran. She's an exceptional architectural beauty," Rachel had said. "She's got it all. Spacious, shady porches, high-ceilinged rooms, jobbed windows, paneled doors, slate hearths and even silver-plated doorknobs. I love every inch of her." Of course, all this praise was before she'd encountered the ghost girl, Trinket Ferguson.

My stomach sank at the sight of Rachel's empty car sitting off to the left side of the driveway. It didn't look like she had car troubles—the tires were intact, the hood wasn't up and nothing appeared to be broken. I immediately began searching the car while the others fanned out to look around. Her keys were in the ignition. The smiley-faced frog dangled there like everything was perfectly fine. My granddaughter was not missing. Nothing was wrong. *Go home, Gran.* In the passenger seat was her quilted purse, but there wasn't much else. The car was neat and tidy, just like Rachel herself.

"Perhaps we shouldn't handle the car too much. You know, in case law enforcement needs to dust it for prints." Bree touched my shoulder and tried to pull me out of the car. I handed her the keys.

"You watch too much television, Bree." My comment stung her, but I didn't care. Rachel needed us!

"Rachel! Rachel!" Bree left me staring at the car and began to walk through the orchard calling for her daughter. I joined her. I needed to stop being an ass—that wasn't helping anyone.

"Rachel-girl! Where are you?"

Soon Rachel's name was echoing around the property; other than a few odd shoe prints that disappeared into the orchard, we didn't find her. That was both encouraging and discouraging. No bits of clothing or obvious signs of a struggle, but then again, no Rachel either. "We need a bloodhound out here. By the time those cops get involved, whatever tracks there are will be washed away. It's supposed to come a gully washer tonight."

Bree didn't engage in conversation with me; she kept calling for Rachel. We heard nothing. Not a peep. "Let's join the others. I think they went inside. There have to be at least fifty rooms in there." My daughter's voice quivered as she continued, "I wish I hadn't done it, Mom. I should never have given up the gift. She needs me now, and I can't reach her."

I put my arm around her and hugged her to me as we walked up the hill. "I have the gift, and it isn't helping me right now. Let's stop blaming ourselves and focus on finding Rachel. Like you said, we'll find her. Uh-oh. Look who's here." We paused and waited for Angus to park his ugly green car. I couldn't make up my mind if I liked this guy or not. Mostly I didn't, but that was because of what I knew. He was bad news and not just because the supernatural went on high alert whenever he was around. Like with Ashland's earlier evasiveness, I felt like Angus was not being completely honest with us all. But then I was naturally suspicious of people. Normally Southern women my age take up tomato growing or fill their lives with cats. Not me. I liked examining people. I liked getting to the bottom of a good secret. And Angus was definitely an enigma. Maybe because he was the first true Scotsman I'd met in Alabama. Why was he here?

"I thought I could help."

"I don't know how much help you'll be. You're a spirit magnet, and we don't need spirits confusing things right now; we need to find Rachel," I barked at him. His face fell, and I followed that up with, "But since you are here, come on." We walked into the house and could hear the others calling Rachel's name.

After searching for what felt like hours, we all gathered downstairs. There were seven of us in all. At least that was a lucky number. Carrie Jo paced while the rest of us sat around the parlor. "Okay, so we know that she's here or she was here."

"No, we know her car is here. Does anybody know for sure that she was actually here?" Ashland asked. Everyone stared at him, and he shrugged. "What? I want to make sure we don't assume anything. Who saw her last?"

"I guess we did," Bree said. "She was going for a drive, but she didn't tell us where she was going. I just figured she needed some space."

Angus cleared his throat. "I asked her to come here but not by herself. I wanted us to explore the house together, do some ghost hunting. She said no and told me to leave. I didn't think she'd go by herself." I shivered as he spoke. Was it getting colder in here?

Nobody said anything for a minute. The tall blonde, Detra Ann, leaned forward and asked him directly, "And you had no idea she was coming to Idlewood? You didn't come with her?"

"I didn't know, and no, she wasn't game for that at all. I mean, we did come here once before, but that was at least six months ago. She wouldn't let me come back and document. This evening I guess I pushed her too hard. I don't know." Detra Ann leaned back, satisfied that he'd been telling the truth.

"What else, Angus?" I prompted him. "Tell them the rest of your story."

"You know?"

"Yes. I'm her grandmother." I didn't feel the need to explain that I'd been eavesdropping on their conversation last night. "Of course she would tell me." Bree's hurt expression went largely ignored by the rest of the group. She picked the wrong time to get sensitive about Rachel. I continued, "Tell them, please. It might help us get into Rachel's head."

"All right, if you think it will help Rachel, but I can't be responsible for what happens."

Henri said, "Wait. Do you mind if I record this? It might help us later." He glanced at Carrie Jo and Angus. Neither objected, so he pressed the record button and we listened to Angus explain his connection to the house—I was hearing this for the second time. He didn't vary his story, not one iota, which did my heart good.

With a sigh of relief he completed his confession. "I'm not proud that I kept who I was a secret from Rachel or any of you, but I didn't want to put anyone at risk. Whatever it was that punched me in the driveway that first day I met Rachel, I have felt it before. It never left me, and I know it all started here."

"Could it be possible that you are somehow kin to the Fergusons? They were from an ancient Scottish clan. It's obvious you are Scottish too. I don't want to assume, but do you know anything about your own history?"

"A little bit, and yes, it could be possible."

Ashland rose first and walked to the window. Naturally all eyes were upon him since he saw ghosts the most often. When he didn't say anything, I slapped my leg and said, "I can't just sit here. Let's search again. We still have a few hours of daylight, and there's a lot of property to cover."

Carrie Jo watched Ashland for a minute, obviously hoping he could add something to the here and now, but he kept his mouth shut. *Fine time to abandon your gift, buddy!* I wished I could see what he saw. Maybe the spirits could point me toward my granddaughter. Well, it couldn't hurt to ask.

"You are right, Jan," Carrie Jo said. "We should look again." She glanced at her watch. "I don't think we have hours, though. More like an hour and a half. The days are so short now."

Henri turned off the recorder and held out his hand to his wife. "Let's go to the garconniere. Rachel was reluctant to go there last night. Maybe she went back to check it out."

"No," Ashland said, his voice low with an edge of warning to it. "Nobody goes to the tower except me. Everyone stay here. I'll be back."

"No, Ashland!" Detra Ann barked at him. "That's not going to happen. We don't go exploring alone. You know that."

"You can't do this, Detra Ann. I have to go by myself. If someone is with me, it's a distraction. There is something here on this property, but it feels different. Real different. It's elusive. I don't know how else to describe it, but it doesn't feel the same. Not ghostlike."

I couldn't help myself. I had to ask the question we were all dying to ask. "Do you see anything? Anyone? Do you see Rachel?"

With a quick sympathetic glance, Ashland shook his head. "No, that's the thing. I see nothing. Nothing at all. Every other time I've been here, this place has teemed with echoes. That's what I feel right before I see a ghost. But now there are no echoes here. No ghosts. It's as if they are hiding."

Sabrina gasped and said, "But from what?" Almost simultaneously everyone cast a suspicious eye on Angus.

Carrie Jo sprang to her feet. "Like heck you're going by yourself. I won't go inside, but I'll at least walk with you down there. And I had a dream about the garconniere. Percy Ferguson's wife was trapped there for a while, in the cellar. That's it! She might be in the cellar!"

"Sorry, Carrie Jo, but Henri and I looked down there. Didn't see her."

"I'm going," she said with a determined voice, her curly ponytail bobbing in defiance.

"No, babe. I've got to do this alone."

She wanted to argue with him again, but Ashland was up and walking toward the door.

Henri dug in the green nylon bag he'd brought in with him. He pulled out a small piece of plastic and flipped a switch, and a red light came on. "Hey, Ash. Take this with you. It's an EMF detector. It might help you spot whatever you're after."

"What does it do?" the handsome young man asked his friend as he accepted the black box. He fiddled with the knob for a second.

"You hold it out like this." He demonstrated by waving the small box with his hand, pointing the little antenna to different areas of the room. "It measures electromagnetic fields. If you notice any fluctuations, it might be an indicator that there's an energy burst around you. That could indicate that a spirit or entity is nearby."

"Got it. Thanks, Henri. Be back in a couple of minutes."

I watched him disappear through the doorway. I hoped he was right.

Chapter Nine—Ashland

The tower apartment didn't appear too intimidating from the top of the hill, as it was only two stories high. But once I walked down the stone stairs, that perspective changed. The garconniere, a fancy name for a 19th-century bachelor pad, was a strange thing to see emerging out of the otherwise scenic landscape. What architect thought this would be the perfect place for a tower? Were there other towers on the property back in those days? We'd probably never know. Perhaps in Old Mobile, it seemed a romantic idea to have a young man dwell in a tower, like a chivalrous knight. Again, how would we ever know? Unless my wife stepped back into the past there in her dreams. Carrie Jo could do that, if she cared to.

And how was I supposed to sleep next to her again knowing that at any time she could see the truth about me? How had she not yet seen my past crime? I couldn't understand it, except maybe grace from above. The guilt weighed on me afresh today, thanks in part to my earlier meeting.

Just past the building was a clump of forbidding trees and beyond them the sunken gardens, resting in perpetual melancholy. Yet these all seemed lively places compared to the building that stood before me. It was as if the garconniere were a lone emblem of the past, forgotten and empty—angry that it had been left behind. It didn't fit here now. It was an empty hull, a dead husk of whatever it had been. Just as all the former tenants in the place were dead husks, buried in deep holes in the ground or laid out in mausoleums until even their bones turned to dust.

But it wasn't truly empty. Not by a long shot.

With every step I took, the anxiety skyrocketed. My imagination helped it along as it ran wild; I believed completely that invisible eyes were watching me, counting my every step, every beat of my heart. To say I was afraid would be an understatement, but I had to try to find our friend. If my examination turned up anything, gave us any clues to Rachel's whereabouts, it would be worth the terror I felt right now. She was just a kid who happened to get mixed up in our strange world. We could not, would not, abandon her to whatever forces were at work here.

My hands felt sweaty, and I shoved Henri's black box into my pocket. Did I really need that thing? I *was* a ghost detector—no batteries required.

As much as I would have preferred to "sneak up" on whatever was in the tower, the thick floor of crunchy magnolia leaves and cast-off seed pods under my feet gave my position away. I might as well have walked up to the door banging a drum or clanging a bell. But as I'd discovered, my supernatural ability did that anyway.

When I was a kid I would never have done this. No matter how many times my mother pleaded with me. And she knew what I could do long before I could appreciate it.

"Please, Ashland. Open your eyes and look for Mother."

I hated when she'd asked me to search for ghosts, which was far too often in those last years; especially when we hung out in the gardens at Seven Sisters. I never wanted to see another thing after those weird séances and visits from greedy psychics. But here I was, the man of the house now, a protective father and loving husband, doing exactly that.

Looking for ghosts. I felt beads of sweat pop out on my forehead, and it wasn't even remotely hot out here.

Yes, I had to do this. Maybe I'd get lucky and the ghost, or whatever hung out here, would just kill me. It seemed better than the alternative, for I faced an impossible situation. I was backed into a corner now, thanks to Jeremy and Libby. Carrie Jo had been right all along. I should never have agreed to have lunch with him today. I had no idea that a trap was being set for me.

Libby was a smart girl. Maybe smart wasn't the right word. Crafty, that was it. She had the evidence she needed now; she could easily convict me of my crimes, at least to my wife. Now I had to pay up or lose the best thing that ever happened to me, both of them. I couldn't imagine my life without Carrie Jo and Baby Boy. That's really what this was all about; why I was here challenging this being. Some would call it living dangerously. The truth was I'd rather die than face the storm that was headed my way.

"All right, you bastard," I shouted to the building as I stood on the porch. Feeling more anger than confidence, I opened the door and stepped inside. It was colder inside than outside. It was not a big space, but it was large enough to entertain a small group of friends, or whatever mischief a bachelor could muster.

Words to live by, right, ol' boy?

What? Those weren't my thoughts! Yes, there was "someone" here, although they remained hidden from view. The big circular room had a few windows, but they were pretty high off the ground. Obviously the Fergusons didn't want anyone peeping in during those wild parties, and I knew by the energy in the room that some "wild" things had indeed occurred here. And now, as though the sun were conspiring against us in favor of the Presence, it appeared much darker outside than it should be. Perhaps it was only the tower? Was there a demonic cloud hanging over the place?

There was just enough light now to cast an amber glow in the room, and I could see streams of dust motes very clearly. They were microscopic galaxies spinning unseen, except by me and by the other being upstairs.

"Rachel!" I called futilely into the empty room. I heard nothing except the shrill beep of the EMF detector in my pocket. I just about jumped out of my skin. I'd forgotten all about the gadget and fumbled to retrieve it while it pelted my ears with another round of alarms. The digital display showed a spinning arrow and fluctuating numbers. I had no idea what any of it meant. I flipped it around a few times looking for an off switch and finally found a slide power button along the side. I turned the thing off with shaking fingers and put it back in my pocket. Breathing a sigh of relief to quiet my breathing, I said in an even, patient voice, "I know you're here. What do you want? Where is my friend?" I took a deep breath and added, "I want to see you. Why are you hiding?"

I heard a crashing sound coming from upstairs like a chair being kicked over. Apparently this thing had a short temper and didn't mind throwing a tantrum. I stood my ground, refusing to run away like that child my mother constantly baited to look for ghosts. *She'd be so proud now.*

"Rachel! Where are you?" No answer came except the emergence of a small shadow, the size of Baby Boy's favorite ball. It bounced down the first couple of wooden stairs in a playful manner and then paused as if it wasn't sure what to do with me, the intruder. Nope, this thing was anything but playful. At least it wasn't Rachel's spirit. This thing was not warm or kind or any of the things she was.

She was still alive!

I stared at the ball, looking for any clue as to who I was dealing with here. I saw nothing but darkness. As the ball swirled in on itself, it expanded and grew quickly to double its size. I stared harder, but it was impossible to see any human-like features. Suddenly the shadow zipped down the stairs, flinging itself against the wall next to the largest window. It flattened and slid up the beams of the roof. The curtains fluttered and settled quietly. It did not move an inch, staying where it was as if to convince me that I could not see it. That it belonged there. It was just a shadow after all.

But I did see it and refused to play along.

"Rachel!" I called again. Nothing else happened; the shadow did not budge, but I knew I wasn't out of the woods yet. I had to check upstairs, just in case she was up there. That was where the thing had come from. It made sense she would be upstairs.

I silently counted to three and on three, I ran across the room and up the stairs. "Rachel!" I called again, half-worried that the ball might follow me. It didn't have to. It was here in the room, looming in front of me, taller and even blacker than it had been before. I swallowed as the murky space began taking shape, and it was the shape of a man I did not recognize.

"I see you…" I whispered to it.

And I see you, Michael...but you'll never have her.

I didn't see the point of talking aloud again. I could hear the voice in my mind; I assumed he could hear me too.

I am not Michael. I want my friend back! Where is my friend? Where is Rachel?

Hissing, he said, *Leave this place, Michael. You will not have her.*

Suddenly a pale face appeared in the center of the dark mist; he had faded, golden hair and pale hands that were reaching toward me. His eyes widened with hatred, so much hatred that they appeared as two burned-out pits with no vestiges of human warmth. Hands, inhumanly long, stretched toward me, and I knew what he meant to do. He was going to push me down the stairs! Or maybe he intended to steal the life from my body by touching me.

He was only a few inches from me now when suddenly the EMF box in my pocket started screaming again. The hands drew back and almost immediately, the ghost fell in on himself, returning to a ball and fading away all in a matter of seconds. I turned off the box again and waited to hear Rachel's voice. She had to be here!

The entity had left and taken the cold with him. The warmth returned to my hands first, and I knew that for the moment I would not get my wish. He would not kill me. I had lived to deal with life another day.

And then I heard her voice, softly, under my feet. "Ashland! Help me! Oh God, help me! I'm here! Please don't leave me here! Help me!"

Rachel was in the floor! I grabbed my phone out of my other pocket and told Carrie Jo that I heard Rachel's voice. She and the rest of the group ran down the hill to the tower, and soon the upstairs room was full of people, tapping on boards and looking for secret doors.

Jan began to cry when she heard Rachel's voice, but we were still no closer to finding her. Angus finally said, "Here! Under the bed, there is a false floor!" The men shoved the heavy oak bed out of the way and sure enough, there was a false floor and a trap door hidden under the bed. Dragging the bed to the side, we opened the trap door and found Rachel crumpled in a ball. Angus scooped her up in his arms and cried as she held him tight. "I'm okay, I'm okay. Please get me home. I have to go home, Angus."

"Yes, Rachel. I'll take you home. I swear I will." Like he was carrying the most precious cargo he'd ever carried, Angus stepped carefully down the stairs and right out the front door with her. Jan was not two steps behind him, and her face said it all. That girl was her life.

Nothing tried to stop him or any of us. I used my spiritual feelers to test the place again, and now there was nothing, it was gone. For some reason, the EMF had frightened it away. I'd have to ask Henri if he'd ever experienced that before. Carrie Jo hugged me and kissed my cheek. I squeezed her and wanted to confess my heart right then and there, but I didn't.

Then Jan hugged me, and I did not stop her although I was in danger of breaking into tears at any moment myself. "Thank you, Ashland. You are a man of honor. I am so grateful to you." Before she released me she whispered in my ear, "Tell her. She'll understand. She'll know what to do."

Shocked into silence, I patted her back and didn't look at her. We left the place, all of us tired and ready to go home. As I was climbing into the car, Sabrina approached Carrie Jo. She thrust a keychain into her hands, squatted beside our car and said to her, "This belongs to Rachel. You've probably seen it before. Please use this to find out what happened to her, CJ. I have to know. I have to know what to do to stop it from happening again. I don't have the gift anymore, and I can't protect her. Please help me protect my daughter."

My wife nodded seriously and shut the door. I knew what that meant. She'd be dreaming tonight. As long as she didn't dream about me, everything would be fine.

But for how long?

Chapter Ten—Carrie Jo

How Rachel got trapped under the floor was a question we would have to ask another day. If a living human was guilty, no doubt the police would be involved, but I wasn't sure that was the case yet. Ashland didn't want to tell me about what he saw, what had happened at the house before we rushed in. But he did agree with me about the police. "She's like a kid sister to us all. We're not going to allow her to be victimized by some crazy person. I mean, sometimes the living work with the dead! How many times have we seen that? Like I said, we just don't know yet. I'll make some calls, but I don't think I have as many friends on the police force as I used to. Except that guy I went to school with, and he's just a beat cop. Maybe that Detective Simmons, you know, the one with the red hair who likes you so much? Perhaps she'd be willing to get to the bottom of it?"

"Simmons? Good luck. Besides, I don't think she's in Mobile anymore, is she? She didn't show up at our last encounter with the cops. Wait…Simmons…Simmons. That reminds me, Austin Simmons came by to see you today. He left his business card at the house. Do you think they could be related?"

"Are you talking about the weird guy who played the piano at the Idlewood presentation?"

"You didn't notice anything else unusual about him?"

"Um, no? Did he have six fingers? Is that why he played like an expert?"

"He looked like David Garrett! Are you blind? Do you have any idea what that's about?"

"Can't think why he'd want to see me; it's you he followed around all night."

"Hardly all night."

His comment stung and I got the impression it was meant to, but I refused to get into an argument with him. He glanced off to his left as he made the turn onto our street. Ashland was doing a remarkable job at hiding his feelings from me. He was in his protective shell, and I was too tired to pull him out of himself. If he got ready to talk, he would; otherwise he could sulk over whatever it was that bothered him. I had a mission, a private mission to dream about Rachel. I felt for the stuffed frog keychain in my pocket. I'd been caught off guard by the request, but I had agreed so I would certainly do it. No arguing there. I loved the girl. "If it's all right with you, I'm going to turn in early. I've got to do something."

"Just say it, Carrie Jo. You have to dream. And you are dreaming to help Rachel. No sense in being vague. Just say it and do it."

"What the heck is your problem, Ashland? Why are you so short with me right now? Have I done something to offend you? Embarrass you?"

"No, it's nothing like that. It's...nothing."

"Fine, it's nothing." He hadn't even really stopped the Jeep before I was jumping out. I couldn't stand to be around him when he was like this. It was awful. I left him behind and walked inside the house. Momma hadn't locked the front door again. I'd have to remind her about that. Again. After her recent accident she seemed more forgetful than ever. Tonight, she'd fallen asleep on the couch with the baby in her arms. I quietly picked up the toys and covered her with a blanket.

I reached for the baby, but she mumbled, "No, let me hold him a little while longer, Carrie Jo. We're okay."

"All right. I'm going upstairs to get a nap myself."

"Okay."

The baby stirred at the sound of my voice, and I quickly exited the room. I planned to hold Rachel's keychain when I fell asleep. I'd dreamed about the living before, so I knew it worked, but it had been a long time since I'd tried.

Luckily, Ashland came in quietly and went straight to his office. *Good! Let him go sulk himself silly. He's a hero, if he'd just know it!*

I settled down in the downstairs guest room, close enough to hear Baby Boy if he started crying, and cuddled up with the soft white down comforter. But he stayed quiet, and soon I got to work.

Rachel, show me what happened. Let me see. See? I have your keychain. I'm here to help. Please let me help you.

I felt my eyes get heavy and I lingered in the in-between, the place in between asleep and awake. I could sense the dream approaching; the honey hues of the dream surrounded me. Then I was there, and this time my heart was racing and I was feeling love, great love. I kept my eyes closed until I was sure I'd crossed over, and then I opened them.

Chapter Eleven—Aubrey

Dashing into the carriage behind Percy, I fell beside him and whimpered as the sound of the barking hounds began to fade behind us. I had no idea who the carriage belonged to, but I did not fret. I was with my own dear love, my golden husband, the keeper of my heart. I wept on his chest as he smoothed my hair and pulled me close.

"It's all right now. We are together, Aubrey. I will never leave you again."

And that was enough. We rode for over an hour, and when the carriage finally came to a creaking stop, we stepped out into the night in front of a small wooden home, a place I did not recognize. "Where are we, Percy? Is this far enough? Will he find us?"

"Hush now. We are safe here. Tomorrow evening, we sail together, away from this evil place. We will start over and be as we once were." I nodded, wanting to believe his promise with all my heart. The carriage disappeared as he stepped inside, and I followed him. Would I ever again allow him to leave my sight? Certainly I would rather die. He searched for matches and soon had a warm glow burning in the fireplace. It was a good thing too. There was a chill in the night air, and rain was beginning to fall. It tapped lightly on the tin roof at first, then began to beat upon it in a steady, comforting rhythm. I breathed a sigh of relief. A good rainfall would most certainly hide us. At least for a little while. I closed the curtains on all the windows. Better to stay hidden from any passerby, but who would find us in this wild place?

There were two rockers before the fireplace, and one held a cozy-looking quilt. It was so inviting that I immediately availed myself of the comfort it offered, hoping to warm up before foraging for food for us both. Perhaps Percy had thought of that too. Was this his place? Had he been only a carriage ride away this whole time? I didn't want to believe that. I couldn't allow myself to think it!

I stared at him as he poked at his fledgling fire. He looked better than when last I saw him. He'd become so thin after Tallulah's death, as if he'd pledged to never eat again. His hair was longer but still bright and almost golden. He let it flow freely around his shoulders. He did not dress as a fine gentleman today; his clothing was threadbare, and the cuffs were obviously worn. I studied his profile as he dusted his hands and sat in the chair beside me. Still as handsome as ever, Percy had a perfect profile. How lucky I'd felt to be married to such an exquisitely handsome man; how jealous my small circle of friends had been! And to think I'd given him up for dead.

Oh God! I have married his brother! Does he know?

I pulled the quilt up to my chin as if it could hide my sin from him.

"Are you cold? It will warm up soon, dearest. Just give it time."

"Percy, how did you know where to find me? I thought I would die down there," I said, my eyes staring at the promised blaze that suddenly erupted into a warming bank of flames.

He stared at the fire too. His tone and cadence changed slightly as he spoke. "I used to have a hound named Jack.

My father gave him to me for my twelfth birthday, and Tallulah kept his sister, Marla. Jack was the runt, but he was smart. Smart as a whip. I loved that dog! He was so loyal that he slept at the foot of my bed every night. One day I came home and Jack was gone. We searched for him for days but never found him. A few months later, my brother revealed to me where I could find the dog. He was shackled in the basement of the garconniere, likely starved to death, or perhaps Michael had beaten him to death. By the time I found him I could not tell, and Michael would never say. I asked him why he would do such a thing, as he'd never expressed an interest in the dog before one way or the other. He never answered me. My father whipped him soundly, but he was unrepentant."

"So you believe Michael would have killed me, like the dog? And so you rescued me?"

"To tell you the truth, I did not know you were there until I entered the place. I heard your voice calling for help."

Crestfallen, I whispered, "You didn't come for me, then?"

"I always planned to come for you, Aubrey, but I'm a man with no name, no fortune, no way to provide for you. How would my retrieval of you help in any way?"

Glassy tears filled my eyes and obscured my view of the fire; only the brightness shone clearly. He didn't know, then. He didn't know what I'd endured, that I married his brother. And he had not come for me.

"Aubrey…" He was suddenly kneeling before me, those beautiful blue eyes looking into my face. His hand gently wiped away the tears. "Had I known you were in danger, that Michael would dare to lift a finger against you, then of course I would have come. I went looking for my papers, something to prove my identity. I don't dare go into the house or he will kill me. I am sorry for the danger I put you in. I am sure he put you there to punish me."

"I thought you were dead," I said in a whisper. "You let me think you were dead."

"No, Aubrey. You knew I was alive. I sent you a letter. I told you where I was and where I was going."

"I received no letter. I thought you were dead."

He laid his head in my lap and cried. "I am sorry, Aubrey. I let you down. I always let down the people I love. You, Tallulah and Dot. Now I hear my mother is dead. Please forgive me. I swear to you upon my own soul that I will not leave you again."

Naturally my heart stirred. Here he was, and he was all I ever wanted. The man I always wanted. "Hush now, my love. We are together now, and that is all that matters. Nothing else matters. Just you and me."

When he stopped crying, he looked at me and we flew into a kiss. Percy's hands were in my hair, then he removed the pins that held the remnants of my previously elegant bun. It cascaded over his hands and he touched it lovingly, not caring that I still smelled of sweat and fear.

And there before the fire on a pallet we made with the quilt, we purged one another of the past, and of Michael and all the pain. We touched each other, kissed and made love until we felt the chill of the evening seep into our bones. Percy stoked the fire, and I wrapped up in the quilt and slipped into the small feather bed stowed in the corner of our humble abode. How wonderful to be free of our prison! To be away from Idlewood!

Percy and I were quiet, not talking much beyond the sweet words that lovers whisper to one another on their pillows in the dark. I would not demand answers from him, not this night and maybe not any other. I never wanted to cause him pain. We were one again as we'd always meant to be— together. Yes! Let the past die and let tomorrow come! For the first time in over a year I welcomed tomorrow, for it would arrive in a happy glow and I would be safe in Percy's strong arms. We would find our way in this world. Together.

Peaceful at last, we fell asleep and I dreamed of nothing. I woke to the sound of squirrels chirping outside our window. The rain had ended, and I could smell the fresh air; my stomach rumbled, but I was happy. I rose, stretching with a huge smile on my face. Percy slept heavily beside me, and I was loath to wake him. Perhaps I could find some fresh eggs nearby or muster up something else for breakfast. I did not know much about cooking, but I wanted to try for him. He needed me. As I went to sling back the covers, I noticed that we were not alone.

Sitting in one of the rocking chairs was Michael!

He wore his black morning suit with a fresh collar and cuffs, and his hair was perfectly arranged. He wore it short and combed neatly. His walking stick lay across his knee, the familiar silver top glinting in the morning light. I noticed that he had not come alone; there was another man outside, and even though I could not see his face, I knew it could only have been the lowly Edward LaGrange. Bridget's husband was the only man allowed to witness the inner workings of Michael's shameful family, as he described us all. Horses snorted in the cold morning air, and I gasped, pulling the covers around me to cover my naked body.

"Good morning, wife."

"I am not your wife," I said as I shoved Percy's shoulder. He woke immediately and sat up in the bed like the devil himself had visited us. Indeed, he had.

"Why are you here?" Percy said, reaching for his pants that hung from the corner post. He wasted no time getting dressed. He courteously handed me my slip, and I put it on without a word.

"Come now; don't be dull, sir. You know exactly why I am here. You have taken my property, and I want it back. And you broke our agreement. Or were you too drunk to remember it, Mr. Sinclair? You aren't to be anywhere near Idlewood or even in Mobile. What happened? Did you spend all your allowance? Is that why you have kidnapped my wife? Hoping to force me to comply with your demands?"

Percy snorted at Michael's words. "You *dare* come here like this! Without even knocking! You do not command me, Michael. And you do not command my wife. You may have stolen my inheritance and my name, but you will have nothing else! Now get out before I thrash you!"

"Oh, it is too late for you to claim her as wife. Or hasn't she told you?" Michael sneered, showing his crooked white teeth. There was nothing pleasant in that smile. He looked like an angry dog. "Now come, Aubrey. There's no need to keep up this farce; it is torture for the man, and anyone can see he is not well. It is time. We must go home." Despite his declaration, he didn't rise up; he must have known I would not easily abandon Percy, that I would fight him at every turn. He knew my love for Percy was eternal and abiding. Nothing he could do would cause my affection to diminish in any capacity.

"Michael, don't," I pleaded with him. "Just go."

Percy glared at him—he was wearing his shirt, suspenders and boots now. He walked to the door and flung it open. "Get out now!" Edward LaGrange tilted his hat at me but gave Percy a look that threatened murder. He did not come inside or make any attempt to drag me out. For that at least I was thankful. My eyes darted about the room. There must be a weapon here—a gun, perhaps. I could shoot a gun!

Michael laughed at Percy and pointed at him as if he were the butt of some huge joke. It was a coarse chuckle at first and then a full-blown fit of laughter. No laughter had ever sounded so sinister and hollow. "But you know, don't you? You already know!" Michael slapped his knee as if he were having the time of his life. "You knew all the time that I was taking her," he said, leering at me, "and you did nothing to stop me."

"Please stop," I said, covering my ears with my hands as if it would prevent the words from stabbing my heart.

"He knew, Aubrey, and he did not rescue you. You will never take her place. He doesn't love you, or else how could he have abandoned you?"

Percy reached for the knife on the wooden dining table. It looked rusty and ridiculously large, but he wielded it as if he meant to use it. Could he defend us from them both? No, he could not! I leapt out of the bed, my feet slapping on the cold wooden floor. I reached for a skillet and stood beside Percy and shivered.

Michael rose now, his smug smile growing as he wiped the tears of laughter from his eye. "He knew, and he did nothing. You can't just abandon your husband, Aubrey. What will people say?" His voice changed, and he whacked the rocker with the wooden stick. It made a ferocious sound, and I jumped instinctively but did not leave Percy's side.

Percy's hand was on my shoulder. "It's all right, Aubrey. Let him say his hurtful words. He can't separate us anymore." I sniffled the heartbreak away and nodded. Michael was evil—surely these were lies. Surely they were!

"You are an evil man. How did you become the creature that you are, Michael?"

Michael took a step toward us, his gaze never leaving Percy's face. He did not answer his brother's question but continued his own script. "You left her quite accommodating, brother, but she's not worth the fuss now. Did she tell you about our little party? She had a few too many drinks and lost her head. And I introduced her to the Creel Society. You remember our motto, don't you? *We brothers share all things...*"

Percy glanced at me and swallowed. "You lie! You are a lying bastard! You will pay for those words."

What could he mean? What did he mean? I couldn't remember. It had been the Creel Society's party I'd attended. Michael had been so excited about it all. He wanted to introduce me to his closest friends. I'd been told what to wear, how to arrange my hair. He'd even purchased new perfume for me. But I'd drunk only one glass of champagne, just one! Flashes of images filled my mind, and I gasped at the memories.

"No! No, Michael!" Even as I denied it, I remembered the truth.

"Aubrey?" Percy asked me, touching my shoulder.

"I can't remember. I woke up in the garconniere, where you found me! I swear it. I don't remember."

Percy stood between Michael and me. "Enough of this! Do you think I will punish her for what you've done? I will not. Leave, brother, and do not show yourself to us again."

Michael's face was a mask of solemnity now. LaGrange stood ready with his gun in hand, but Michael waved him away. He walked toward the door, and I thought for a moment we'd be free. Free forever. But he had to deliver the last wound to Percy, a wound that would never be healed.

"But what about Tallulah? Is she forgotten?"

"What are you talking about now, fool?" Percy waved the rusty knife at him, but Michael didn't move. He positioned his hat on his head perfectly and stroked his mustache.

"Percy," I warned him, "make him leave, please. I beg of you."

"She wrote to our sister while you were gone. She explained to her how displeased you were with her refusal to marry Mr. Chestnut and how you did not wish to receive any more correspondence until she became his dutiful wife. But Tallulah could not stomach him. He was a distasteful man. Not worthy of taking a Ferguson wife. But your own sweet wife relayed in great detail your demeanor concerning the whole scandalous affair. She made sure our Golden Sister climbed that tree. But surely it was your dictation that she penned, your words that she wrote?"

Percy's confusion was apparent. "More lies. Is nothing sacred? She was your sister too. How dare you accuse Aubrey of conspiring in such an evil plot..." Percy's words were less of a statement and more a question, and I knew it was over. The dream of love lost and found would end at this moment.

I felt the room spinning. I'd forgotten that my arms were bare and that my feet were cold—I no longer cared. I sat in a nearby chair, still clutching the skillet. But I would not use it now. I'd been defeated, my secret revealed. I could never take back the words or the deed, and Percy would never forget the insinuation. Even if I could muster the skill and strength to lie to him, it would do no good. And after all I'd been through, I could not. What was the expression the old folks say? "The twisting of the leaf reveals the worm beneath."

"Aubrey?" Percy lowered his blade and faced me. "He's lying. Tell him he's a liar."

Michael paused and waited for my response. What could I say? My unbound hair fell around my face, and I slowly raised my head. This was the moment that I'd dreaded. For an entire year I dreaded this, and now it was upon me.

With no more laughter, Michael made to leave. "And so I will leave you as I found you. Please do not return to Idlewood. Either of you."

Percy paced the floor. At long last he dropped the knife, but he was a broken man. He sat on the edge of the bed.

"Tell me why, Aubrey. Why would you do that? Why would you write such a lie?"

I sniffed as I grasped the skillet. "Because she would never let you go if I didn't. I did it for us, Percy."

He wept, and I felt my heart harden at the sound. He cried and cried, but not for me. He cried for Tallulah. "Oh, my Tallulah! My sister!" As he ignored me and spiraled again into his own misery, I gathered my clothing and dressed myself. I did not bother fixing my hair. I left Percy in the cabin and began walking down the long road that would take me to Idlewood. I walked a whole day. By the time I made it back I was near exhaustion, but I had one last task to do.

It was easy to find a rope. The old barn was only a hundred feet away from the tree. I grabbed the nearest one and dragged it behind me; it felt heavy and dirty, but that didn't matter now. I was not much good at climbing trees, but I could surely manage to climb this one once. It was the largest tree on the property with a thick gray trunk and thick branches, more than capable of bearing my weight. I was not as tall as Tallulah and much smaller. I threw the rope into the air a few times before I caught the branch. Oh yes, this was easy. It was as if some unseen force guided me along, helping me achieve my goal. Evening out the rope so it wouldn't slip from the branch once I climbed up, I examined the trunk to discern the path upward. It was not difficult to detect. I set out about stepping up on the worn knot, the same knot I'd seen Tallulah use to get a foothold up the side of the ancient oak one afternoon. I liked spying on her. I wanted to move like her, laugh like her, be like her.

And now I would die like her. Perhaps then Percy would understand the depths of my love. Perhaps with this one act I could take her place, finally take her place, as I had tried to in life. So let it be in death. Without fear I climbed higher until I reached the branch. It took me a while to get the noose tied correctly. It wasn't a very good noose, but it would have to do. Hopefully I would die quickly and not belabor the deed with hours of strangulation or days of merciless starvation. I felt nearly starved now, and I noticed that my hands were quite pale and bony.

I slipped the noose about my neck and thought of what words I should say to Heaven Above.

In the end, I thought of nothing appropriate and so, very easily, I slid off the branch like a bag of salt falling to the ground.

Chapter Twelve—Rachel

My apartment was where the garage used to be, so I heard Carrie Jo's vehicle before she ever made it to the front bell. I was kind of glad I could beat her there because Gran had decided to update the doorbell yesterday. Instead of the gentle dinging we'd heard for umpteen years, it was now an annoying buzzer that surely made visitors think they were on a cheap game show. She also installed a wireless security system, set cameras around the perimeter of the house and purchased all three of us one of those goofy alert necklaces. If you saw a "threat" you could hit the button, then an alarm would go off and the cops would come. My old room, which Gran intended to transform into her art studio, was now security central. I tried to tell her she was overreacting; it was silly to spend her pension on this stuff, but she wouldn't have it any other way. I gave up.

I knew what was going on with her. I mean, I understood why she'd gone off the deep end. That didn't make it any better. Her response to our current situation made it worse. At least for me. I'd never seen anything shake her confidence or steal her joy. Gran felt guilty, plain and simple. But the truth was she couldn't protect me. How can you protect anyone from the spirit world? Spirits have a mind— and agenda—of their own. They do their own thing and follow laws we can't begin to understand. As much as it frightened me, I couldn't put the genie back in the bottle. How do you unknow something?

"Hi!" I said, faking cheerfulness as I opened the door. Carrie Jo seemed relieved to see me. Juggling her son, diaper bag and purse like a pro, she hugged me and managed to hand me a bag of donuts from Ladd's.

"So glad to see you, Rachel. It's only been two days, but it feels like forever. I brought your check, and AJ here insisted that we bring you some donuts. I got crullers!"

"I'll gladly accept both of those. Come on in, guys, and thank you, Baby Boy. They're my favorites! I've got sodas in my mini-fridge. Let's hang out in my room. I don't think you've seen it yet. It's more like an apartment. I love it! And I actually cleaned it up this morning." Normally we'd chat in the living room or maybe the kitchen, but I didn't want Gran overhearing what I had to say. She was stressed out enough.

We arranged a play area for Ashland Junior, then CJ and I sat at the little table I'd placed in the corner of my room. The baby was having a good time investigating all my stuffed animals. "You look good, Rachel. How are you doing? Be honest."

"Me? I'm okay, but I think Gran's gone crazy. She's up in Mission Control right now. Watching the cameras, I guess. I'm surprised she hasn't assigned us all passwords and installed a moat. I keep telling her that the danger isn't here, it's at Idlewood, but she won't listen. That's so weird too because I've never known her to be scared of anything. Mom is working double shifts again, probably so she doesn't have to talk about what happened, and I keep having dreams of Idlewood."

"I'm sorry to hear that. That doesn't sound like your grandmother at all."

I dug in the white bag from Ladd's and arranged napkins on the table. I wasn't going to eat three crullers, so I gave CJ one and put one on my napkin. It smelled delicious.

"You know I have to ask. What kind of dreams?" Carrie Jo's green eyes studied mine.

"That's the thing. It's only pieces, but they are very vivid. I'm running through the woods, and I can feel the briars tugging at my skin. My feet are cold, and I hear the sound of dogs howling. They frighten me—I mean, the dream me. In real life I'm not afraid of dogs at all. I'm a huge dog lover, but in my dream it is a different story. It's like I'm...well, I'm not even me." I picked up one of the donuts and took a bite. Yep, this is what I needed to do—stress eat.

"Sounds like you've been dream catching. Or maybe you're having those dreams because someone is trying to communicate with you. I've been reading up on sensitives and mediums. That's a common experience for people who have that kind of gift. But then again, maybe you are just a late-blooming dream catcher." She smiled and cracked open the soda bottle I offered her.

"Wouldn't that be something?" After taking a few bites and wiping my face with a napkin I added, "I know who's been crying in the house. It's Aubrey."

"How do you know it's her? I thought perhaps it was Mrs. Ferguson. Or maybe Bridget."

"I have no facts to present, but I believe it's Aubrey. She's so distraught, so heartbroken. Maybe I'm wrong. I think the more I learn the less I know." Baby Boy squealed with delight when he realized one of my bears lit up and played a tune. I couldn't help but smile. Such a happy baby. I hoped he'd have a happy life. You couldn't predict that, though. *Geesh, Rach. What a depressing thought!* "It's sad to think a person's soul could be trapped in a place or in a time like that. Why do you think some people become ghosts and others don't, even though they experience a comparable amount of heartache?"

She shook her head and said, "That's definitely one of life's mysteries. I wish I knew."

We didn't talk for a while but listened to Baby Boy talk to himself in his own sweet, baby language. Or maybe he was talking to Mr. Giraffe and Pinky Elephant, my two childhood favorites. Now it seemed like they were his too. I might as well let him take them home.

"I've been dreaming of Idlewood, Rachel. It's been a few months since I dreamed of the house, but now it's becoming clearer, there's much more detail. I saw Aubrey, Percy and Michael. I know how it ends for her. At least I'm pretty sure. It's not a fairy tale ending."

"Tell me, what happened? I need to know."

Carrie Jo paused for a moment and ran to AJ just in time to keep him from pulling the lamp off my nightstand. "I'm so sorry. I think he's headed to the terrible twos, and he's not even one yet." We rearranged things, and although he wasn't happy about it, he went back to playing with his pile of toys. Once his attention was averted, we went back to our conversation. I noticed CJ lowered her voice as if Baby Boy could understand what she was saying. I guess when you deal with the supernatural all the time, you have to be concerned about that sort of thing. She spilled her secrets and told me about Aubrey's imprisonment and Michael's cruelty. And Percy's indifference. I could hardly believe it.

"Some might say she deserved it, but how could Aubrey have known what Tallulah would do? We saw the letter. Nowhere in there does it suggest that she do such a thing. No wonder Aubrey's haunting the place. If she was trying to show me that, then why was I locked in a completely different room? I wasn't locked in the cellar. I was in the second-floor trap, which I'd never heard of until this house. Have you heard about any others?"

"It's an uncommon feature, for sure, but not unheard of. Especially during the Civil War, which would have been about ten years earlier. It could have been built in to hide soldiers or maybe even slaves. Can you tell me how you ended up there? Do you think it was a ghost?"

"No, I don't." My answer surprised her. "I went to the gar-conniere because I wanted to cleanse the place. I wanted Angus to be free, even though I was ticked off at him for trying to manipulate me. I went inside and lo and behold the lights weren't working, again. That's when I knew something was up. I was just about to leave when I heard a noise coming from upstairs. It was like a whisper, like two people talking to one another. I called out to warn them, but nobody answered."

"You should have left and called the cops, Rachel!"

"Hindsight is twenty-twenty, isn't it? I wasn't thinking straight. I'd just got into this big blowout with Angus, and I was still ticked off. So I waited for a while and didn't hear anything. I pretended to close the door but nothing. I went up to check it out. The bed was moved, the floor trap open. How could we have missed it? I could hardly believe what I saw. I swear I didn't see anyone. I peeked inside, thinking that whoever was digging around up there was still inside.

Next thing I know someone shoved me, and hard. I tried to get out, but before I could get my bearings they were gone and the bed was on top of me."

"Oh my lord, Rachel. You could have been...I mean, what if we'd never found you?"

"Stop that, Carrie Jo. If you cry, I'm done. It's bad enough Gran is losing it; you can't go crazy too."

She jumped out of her chair and hugged me before sitting back down. "You know, when Terrence Dale and Bette left us, I thought I would die. I can't imagine what my life would be like without you in it. You are so sweet and special. Like the little sister I never had. Please be safe going forward. No more solo field trips. If you want to investigate anything, you call on one of us. I mean it."

"I'm glad to hear you say that because I have to go back. I need to go back. If there is any possible way to help Aubrey rest, then I need to do it."

"But what if it's not Aubrey? Ashland seems to think it was a male spirit in the tower, not a female one. What if you make contact with the Shadow Man? Whoever or whatever that thing is. What then?"

I chewed the inside of my lip thoughtfully. "With Trinket we knew the letter was the key. Maybe it will work for Aubrey. If I could let her know we'd found it, that she was forgiven..."

"That's just it, Rachel. We don't know that Percy did forgive her. The last time I saw them, he'd basically turned his back on her and she was in Tallulah's tree."

"It's not a science—and I'm probably grasping at straws here, but I've got to do something. I can't sleep. I can't stop thinking about her. It's like an obsession."

"You aren't the first to feel that way." She picked up AJ, who was now fussing and not smelling as sweet as he had when he arrived. "Tell you what. It's probably not going to happen tonight; Ashland's having a football party, and the Devecheauxs stay so busy that it's not always easy to connect with them. Let me see if I can arrange for us all to be there tomorrow night. We work better when we are together, and it is always safer that way too. Also, that will give me some time to think up something to tell Mr. Taylor. If he rode by and saw all those cars there, he'd freak out."

"That's all I can ask for. In the meantime, I'll do some research online, see what I can figure out about helping Aubrey. Henri gave me a tip on a great search engine that might come in handy."

"Great! Well, I hate to do this to you, but my son has decided to make a mess. If I could change him before we head home? It's almost nap time."

"Sure, I'll let you and Mr. Smellypants take care of business. Thanks for stopping by."

"No problem. We love you, Rachel."

"Love you too." I exited the room and went in search of deodorizing spray and a grocery store bag. I loved that little guy, but he was not leaving his "present" in my room. By the time I dug out what I needed from the kitchen supply cabinet, Carrie Jo was walking in behind me.

"Thank you, Aunt Rachel. We'll go home now. Say bye bye, AJ."

After tidying up, I helped her to the car and added the stuffies to the back seat.

"You can't give away your keepsakes. That's above and beyond the call of duty."

"It's not a problem. I think it's time to let a few things go. See you later. Call me when you know something!"

"You got it!" I watched them drive away and waved goodbye. I turned around and almost screamed my head off. Gran was standing right behind me.

"Good Lord, Gran. You scared the daylights out of me. Where did you get those ninja skills?" I laughed nervously.

"Don't go back, Rachel-girl. There's only sadness there. Please don't go back." She didn't wait for me to answer or explain myself. With slumped shoulders and a tired expression, she left me to return to her security room.

I didn't follow her.

Chapter Thirteen—Carrie Jo

The plan was to go home, put my son down for his usual afternoon nap, decorate for the party and help Doreen finish up the food. But Ashland James had other ideas. He wasn't ready for a nap, and he didn't have any intention of letting me put him down. I checked his forehead, and he wasn't feverish, just fussy. After a quick phone call to Momma, who immediately offered to come over, I realized that it was probably teething issues. I rubbed my finger on his gums and was surprised to feel two sharp nubs poking out of his gum line. I told Momma not to worry but reminded her about today. Hey, since I'd forgotten about the shindig myself, I figured I needed to remind my family and friends.

It was the Alabama-LSU game, and the rivalry was in full swing in our neighborhood. Naturally, my huge Crimson Tide fan husband had an oversize Alabama flag hanging off the front porch. I didn't make a fuss about it. Henri was an LSU fan all the way, and those two were certain to give each other a hard time about every play. It would be much-needed relief from the crazy world we often found ourselves in.

"It's official. My kiddo has teeth! I wonder where Ashland is…he said he would be here to help." I stole a few crackers off Doreen's tray, and my son tried to take them from me.

"I have it under control, and my granddaughter Mattie promised to come by and help. You take care of that be-be. It's okay, Mrs. Stuart."

"Are you sure?"

"Yes, very sure. In fact, I might get more done without your help." She grinned, bobbing her head at me.

"All right, then. I'll take him up for some quiet time and see if I can't talk him into a nap. He's so cranky today." I climbed the stairs with the wriggling handful, and we went into his room. I put him in pajamas and let him play on the floor for a few minutes while I put his clothes away. Doreen had brought them up for me, but I liked folding his things and tucking them away. At least I had the opportunity to do that for my son. My mother never had that with Chance.

Where are you, brother? I daydreamed about him as I slipped onesies and pajamas in their proper place. AJ began crying, and I picked him up, suddenly worried that something was seriously wrong with him. It wasn't like him to fight sleep. Unlike some kids, my boy was always down for a nap. Even the ladies at Small Steps commented on how easy it was to get him to sleep. The problem was he didn't always sleep too long.

"It's okay, Baby Boy. It's okay. Come sit with Momma. Let's sit right here in our chair." I sat in the padded rocker/glider that Ashland had surprised me with the night of our baby shower. It was the most comfortable chair in the house and believe me, I should know—I spent enough time in it. "Come on now. Let's lie down here." I rocked him back and forth and hummed whatever tunes I could think of. We started with "Hush, Little Baby" and ended up with "Twinkle, Twinkle Little Star." He didn't seem to mind that his mother was the world's worst singer, that she couldn't carry a tune in a bucket. That she frequently forgot the words and had to make up her own lyrics. Nope, he didn't mind at all. After a few minutes of restlessness, he snuggled down and got still. I didn't dare lay him down too soon. Ashland James was the reigning champion of "playing possum." Just when you thought he was asleep, that blond head would pop up again. I kept humming and rocking, humming and rocking until soon, both of us were sleeping.

***

My chest burned, my feet were freezing. I'd managed to lose my shoes somewhere along the way, but I could not allow that to stop me. The sun hovered on the horizon and threatened to dip below the distant fence line and plunge me and the entire countryside into darkness. All I needed was a little more time, please God, a little more time to find my wife. To hold her, to keep her safe from the Devi—my brother. I'd followed Aubrey's footsteps to the edge of the road, and there could be no doubt now she *was* returning to Idlewood. But for what purpose, I could not imagine. In spite of Michael's warning, she was returning to him. *And what choice did she have if I had abandoned her yet again?* Oh yes, I was a supreme coward. Abandoning those I loved during their time of need was what I did best.

I do not know how long I lingered in the McFarlands' cabin after Michael's visit. I could not even say when Aubrey departed. Could it have been today? Yesterday? Time seemed unimportant to me now. At times in my world Tallulah still lived, my Dot haunted my every step—her serious, scolding eyes were always upon me—and now my Aubrey was in danger of falling into the darkness along with them.

I could hear my brother's taunts in my mind even now. "Ah yes, Sir Percy, the Golden Son. You are a failure, my Golden Brother. You are not my father's son or my brother." Yes, there were far worse taunts than that, but I did not care to recall them now. I wanted to be rid of him forever. But now I had to find my Aubrey. Time would not stand still for us. Time was never on my side.

I paused at the fence, but only for a few seconds. I climbed each of the wooden slats carefully, and my nearly numb toes had a difficult time discerning where to step. I finally crested the fence, stepped over the side and fell to the ground. There were stickers here, tough viney ones, but I couldn't slow down my pace. I rolled out of the briar patch, tearing my skin as I went. When I could finally stand I did. I scanned the horizon to get my bearings. I could see Idlewood in the distance. Purple shadows fell on the side of the house, and soon the gas lamps along the drive were lit by one of the house servants. The growing sense of urgency increased to levels that threatened to put my mind in an ill state again, back to the land of dark clouds and suffering. The catch in my side got worse as I scrambled up the hill, but I didn't dare stop now.

A strange sound caught my attention. I had a choice, run for the house or turn to address this oddity. No, oddity was the wrong word. It was more like an omen.

It was late October now, or was it November? I could not remember, but it was getting colder by the minute. Yet that sound gnawed at me. I decided to circle back, not across the fence but to the old barn. The place where Tallulah and I witnessed the Bad Thing that we never spoke about to anyone, even one another. And now the place of the Bad Thing was calling me back. Maybe it believed that we *had* spoken, that we had told someone, but we had not. I would not forget her eyes as I pressed my hand over her mouth. Tallulah wanted to scream and so did I, but to do so would have meant certain death. Uncle Preston's blood filled the floor of the barn as Father drove the ax into him again and again. He muttered a string of profanities as he delivered each blow, and many of the words I had never heard before.

Buggering bastard! Buggering bastard! Buggering bastard!

When the savagery finally ended, Tallulah had wet her dress and I was unable to stop trembling. And I could not forget the words, "Buggering bastard!"

But it wasn't the barn door creaking. I could see the barn door. It was closed just as the hayloft was. Still the sound was very near now.

Creak, creak. Creak, creak, creak.

There was no rhythm to the noise. I couldn't place it. Until I remembered where I was. This was our place and that was our tree.

And there was a body hanging from the tree. I fell to my knees as the first thought coalesced in my mind. "Tallulah!" But it was not Tallulah. That was not blond hair but brown. And that was not Tallulah's yellow dress but a dress of burgundy, Aubrey's favorite color. I shot back up from the ground.

"No!" I said to the swinging woman. "No!" I walked toward her now, her face hidden from me because of her long, loose hair. I touched her feet. They were stiff and cold, like mine but not like mine. My feet did not yet walk in the land of the dead. "Aubrey, please. Come down from there. Please, my wife. Come down. I will get you down, my love." I scrambled up the tree, for I knew where all the knots were. I'd been climbing this tree since I was a little boy, barely old enough to be away from my mother. This had been our tree, mine and Tallulah's. We'd sworn to never play in the barn again, but here—here we could see the clouds in the day and the stars at night.

And after today, I would never visit this place again. Never. I untied the rope and eased my wife's body to the ground. I returned to her side, unbound the evil rope from her neck and held her lifeless body to mine. I wept over her, calling her back to me, but she was beyond me now. Again I had failed.

This had been my fault. I should have pleaded with Aubrey, explained to her about the Bad Thing and how that secret had kept Tallulah and me together. I should have told her how I had to watch over my sister to keep her from telling the world about the sin of our father—and later, as we surmised the truth, the sin of our uncle. The dark descended on us and the stars shone down upon us, two lovers, now separated by death. I kissed her cheek, but I knew there was no hope. My agony was complete. Then the rage came, black and full of fire and shadows. I welcomed it with all my being. And in the dark under the giant oak I had another moment of crystal-clear clarity. I alone did not bear the weight of all this.

Michael's jealousy, his great envy of me, had driven us all to destruction. For I understood it all now. It was Michael whom Uncle Preston had mistreated, and he hated me for that. He hated the Golden Son, as he liked to call me and taught others to call me. He'd forced me from my home and stolen my inheritance and my wife. And he had killed her. He murdered her with his immeasurable jealousy.

And now he must pay. He must be brought to heel. I picked up Aubrey's body and walked up the hill. I felt no pain, and although the grief was great it evolved into brutish anger. I set my head down and kept my eyes focused on the door of the house. The servants saw me first; I heard them call the Master of the House. Perhaps if I had come alone, penniless and begging, they would have had the courage to shoo me away. But I did not come penniless and begging. I brought with me the greatest thing a man could ever have, a loving wife. I did not brook a word from any of them, and they moved out of the way. They even opened the door for me.

Michael was half-dressed and bounding down the stairs. "Here now, fellow! See here, Sinclair. You are not allowed here. Shamus, call the sheriff!" He grinned at the sight of Aubrey's dead body. With her head flipped back now you could see the raw stripe the rope left, but that did not move him. "Tell him that someone dumped some rubbish on my property and I want it removed."

His words lit the fuse. A fuse that would not be put out with any mortal instrument. I laid my wife's body on the settee and removed my belt. To his utter surprise I slung the belt and slapped him in the face. The first blow landed him on the ground, but he did not stay there. He would wish that he had by the time I was done with him. He struck me a few times in the beginning, but once the red wash of rage poured over my mind I could not control my desire to kill him.

"Buggering bastard! Buggering bastard!" I shouted and screamed as I pounded him with my fists and anything else I could get my hands on. Mr. Lofton and another man dragged me off him, and I stared at him pitilessly as he spit blood, his face a battered slab of meat.

"Please, sir. No more," Mr. Lofton whispered in my ear. "Go now, before the sheriff arrives. Run, sir. Run away."

"No, Lofton. The time for running is over. This family has many crimes to answer for. It is time for a reckoning."

"Please, Master Percy. Think of your sister, Bridget. Please don't do this." To my surprise, the old man's pleas softened my heart. Yes, there was still one soul that I could care for. I would make sure my brother paid for his crimes, and I would pay for mine, but Bridget, she would be cared for no matter what I had to do. How poorly I had treated her all her life.

Mrs. Potts and some other women carried my brother to his bed upstairs, and I sat on the settee with Aubrey's head in my lap. I waited until dawn for the sheriff to return. And when it came time to release her, I cut a lock of her hair to keep with me always.

My sweet Aubrey, she'd been a fool, but I'd forced her to play on. I loved her, not like I should have, not until it was too late. But I loved her. And now she'd never know.

I would never see her again.

***

"Babe, wake up. It's all right, wake up."

I jumped out of the chair in a panic. I realized that Baby Boy was missing. "He's fine. He's asleep. Let's go outside into the hallway."

I followed Ashland out to the hall and immediately slid down the wall and cried. He sat on the floor next to me and let me cry my eyes out. When I could talk, I told him what happened.

"You're kidding me. Poor Aubrey. What a sad place."

"It's not Michael at the garconniere, Ashland. It's not. It's Percy! His hatred has him trapped."

"Hatred for Michael?"

"Some of that hatred is for Michael, but it's also hatred for himself. He's not forgiven himself. He still thinks he's protecting Aubrey in that garconniere. That's why he kept Rachel's whereabouts from you."

"Do you think he put her in there? Seems like a difficult task for a ghost."

I accepted the handkerchief he offered me. "No, I don't. I think the ghost had human help, but darned if I know who. Maybe we will never find out."

"Oh, I think we will. Those kinds of secrets have a way of coming out."

"Yes, they do." I leaned my head on his shoulder.

He sighed and said, "I have a secret I've been keeping, and I don't feel good about it."

I picked my head up off his shoulder and asked, "What secret, Ashland?"

"I've been keeping a secret from you, and I can't do it anymore." He sighed with relief, but that didn't make me feel any better. The other shoe was about to drop.

My heart felt like Percy's now, like it floated in my chest and threatened to drop to my feet. "Stop it, babe. You are scaring me."

"I'm sorry, Carrie Jo. I've been looking for a way to tell you for a while. You were right about Libby. There was a time when we were together—"

"I don't think I want to hear this."

"I have to tell you. If I can tell you, she can't hold it over us anymore and we can move on."

"I don't need to hear this, Ashland." I jumped up and ran to our room. I sat on the bed and stared out the window. It was dark outside—hey, didn't we have a party to go to? Oh my Lord! The party was here! I could see cars pulling into our driveway. Ashland followed me into the room and closed the door.

"You better get dressed for the party," I said, not looking him in the face. I'd pulled my hair up in a side ponytail and tied an Alabama ribbon to it. I practically tore off my shirt—man, I was angry. And I was breaking my promise to myself not to talk about it.

"You are a class-A jerk, Ashland Stuart! I was never unfaithful to you! How could you do this?"

"Oh God, Carrie Jo! No, that's not what I meant. I didn't cheat on you—I would never do that. This was before I met you. I got drunk at a frat party, Libby was there, she was underage, but Jeremy had snuck her into the party. I was blitzed and not thinking clearly. I slept with her, and the next day I didn't even know I had done it. Until Jeremy called the other day and said he had pictures from that night. She'd taken pictures of me, Carrie Jo. I knew if you saw them you'd leave me. She threatened to use the pictures as proof I'd been harassing her all her life. She's still after my fortune, a fortune I no longer have. And more than that, she wants to destroy me. Now she's gotten involved with some legal group called the Creel Society..."

"Creel Society? Oh my goodness, Ashland. You need to call Austin Simmons. He wanted to talk to you about those people. He called today and said he had a word of caution for you. He must know something about what they are up to! Please swear to me that you will call him."

He sat on the side of the bed, his head in his hands. "So you aren't angry at me? You aren't going to leave me?"

"Heck no. In fact, I'm tempted to kick her ass again! What you did before me, was, well, before me. Like me and William Bettencourt. I'm sure you don't want to know how we..."

"You are damn right I don't want to know. And I don't want to hear his name again."

I stood in between his legs and put my arms around his neck. "Did you think I was that shallow? That I would hate you for something you did in high school or college? Please! I'm a grown woman and a real woman. There's nothing Libby Stevenson could tell me about you that I don't already know. I love you, blockhead. Now we're going to miss our party. Unless I can go down in just my bra..." I started heading for the door.

"Don't you dare!" He pulled me to him and we kissed. We were tempted to make the guests wait, but that would be too obvious. We weren't going to behave badly with people in the house. That was just for weddings and large parties.

"I will never be unfaithful Carrie Jo. Never. I am sorry I was ever with her. Believe me, I am sorry. Please forgive me."

"I do forgive you, Ashland. Now let's go party!" I slid on my red and white shirt—it looked great with my blue jeans—and I grabbed my pom-poms. "I'm ready to yell, 'Roll Tide!'" I shook the pom-poms at him, but then the baby woke up and started hollering from his room. People were talking downstairs, and I thought I heard my mother's voice too.

I offered Ash my pom-poms. "These or the baby? Which do you want?"

"Um, I'll take the baby. No way I'm going down there with a pair of pom-poms."

"Good idea! See you downstairs!" Feeling happier than I had in a long time, I bounded down the stairs and greeted our house full of guests. The decorations looked great. My mom spotted me looking at them, and I gave her a thumbs-up. She returned it with one of her own.

I was sorry for what happened to Percy and Aubrey, and Tallulah and Dot. And in a way, I was sorry for what happened to Michael. But that wasn't my life. I had a good life. A happy life.

I never wanted to forget that.

Chapter Fourteen—Rachel

"She said meet her here at eleven? Seems kind of late, considering what you've been through already."

"Okay, *Gran*. Thanks." Angus sure knew how to worry over me like an old lady. "I just want to go inside, speak to Aubrey and tell her to leave. I've got the letter that started it all right here. That should be all we need."

"Why would you need a letter?"

"Well, it's like a trigger. Something that mattered to her in life. If I told you the whole story you'd understand."

"Tell me, then," he said with a sexy smile. "I've got nothing but time right now. Unless you'd like to do something else?"

"You pick now to swing that on me? As if I'd want our first time together to be in the car? Gross."

"Oh, so you *have* thought about it."

I stared at him incredulously. "Am I dead? Of course I think about it. It just seems you aren't too interested in doing that."

"Balls on that. I am very interested, but I've never made out with an American girl before. I wasn't sure what the protocol was. There are no men in your family, no one I can ask for your hand."

"Whoa there. We're talking about having sex, not getting married."

"Not where I'm from." Ah, so that explained it. What had I gotten myself into? Was I dating a purist who believed in sex only after marriage? It was actually kind of sweet.

"I don't always live right, but I try."

"You don't seem too religious to me." Was he putting me on?

"That's the thing, I'm not real religious at all. It's not about religion, it's about a code of conduct that I live by. I believe in honor."

I snorted a laugh. "And that's why you left me that first day at Idlewood."

"I said I believe in it—I don't always get it right."

I laughed and watched Carrie Jo's Beamer pull up. She had Ashland with her, and love must have been in the air because they were kissing passionately as soon as she parked. Hmm…maybe marriage wasn't such a bad thing after all.

"Let's roll, ghost hunter," I said with a wink. He stole a kiss from me, and we stood outside my car, stomping our feet to warm up. "Man, who turned down the thermostat! I believe it could snow, it's so cold. Come on, y'all!"

"Coming!" They got out of the car, and the four of us walked up to the house.

"Anyone else coming?"

"No, it's just us tonight. Henri and Detra Ann had something else they had to do. I have agreed to let him ghost hunt the house, but if he puts it on his website he has to call it an undisclosed location. And I had another dream about what happened. Let's go inside the tower, as Ash calls it, and light a fire. I'll tell you what I know."

I smiled at her, finally feeling that everyone would be okay. She wouldn't lead me wrong, I knew that. Soon the fire warmed us and we sat around the table listening to Carrie Jo tell us about her dream. Unlike some folks, CJ knew how to tell a story. It was as if she were truly there seeing it all; it was very convincing. Chip never believed her, but he was always an unbeliever in the supernatural. More's the pity.

After hearing the entire sad story, I cried. Yet I felt peace. CJ's dream had brought me peace. Aubrey was not here; I had been wrong. It was Percy who needed our help! I walked around the room trying to feel Percy or Michael or Aubrey.

I started talking to the air, and my friends let me. "Percy, I have something of yours. See it? It's a braid of Aubrey's hair. I found it in the attic of the house. It was in her trunk. Can you see it? I'm going to put it right here so you can look at it." Angus took out his EMF pod and put it near the braid. Then he spoke too.

"Percy, my name is Angus. We are here to help you. If you can hear me, beep the pod once." Immediately the pod beeped once. "Okay, Percy. Just to be sure it's you and not someone else, beep twice if you were married to Aubrey." And the pod beeped twice. Angus sat down, looking pleased with himself.

Ashland whispered to him, "I can see him, and that's not Percy. It's Michael; he's standing by the box."

"Oh. Michael, my friend Ashland can see you. You can't trick us, Michael. If that's you, beep twice." The pod beeped twice.

"Michael, you did some bad things in your day. Why are you still here? Do you feel guilty that you caused Aubrey's death?" Suddenly the pod began beeping nonstop, and then it flew off the table.

"That was very naughty, Michael." Angus picked up the pod and put it back on the table.

"Ow!" I shouted as I stared at my arm. "Something scratched me. Michael, did you scratch me?" The machine beeped twice and then three more times. "All right, Michael, calm down. We need to talk with Percy. Can you move away from the pod so we can talk to Percy? Oh!" I pointed at the stairs. There was Percy; his features were faded some, but I knew it was him. He had the same golden blond hair, the slender build, the long fingers. He was a handsome man, even in death.

"Let me talk to him, please, Rachel."

"Sure, Carrie Jo, but be careful."

"Percy? Can you come talk to me? Michael has left so we can talk. Can you make the pod beep so I can see that we are communicating?" The pod beeped, and we all—yes, all four of us—saw him move toward us slowly.

"Percy? Aubrey wants you to know that she has forgiven you for not telling her about the Bad Thing." Immediately the ghost put his head in his hands, and although I could not hear him, I knew he was crying. "She knows, Percy, and she loves you. Now is the time to go to her. Do you want to see Aubrey again?" He made the pod beep once for a long time.

"I know, I know, Percy. It was wrong what was done to you. It was wrong, but now it is time to move on. Time to go be with Aubrey and Tallulah and Dot. Would that make you happy?" The pod gave another long beep. "See the braid? We have her braid here. You can touch it and come see it. It is yours." We saw nothing happen with the braid, but he moved in closer before he disappeared. His face remained serious and unhappy.

"Percy, Rachel is going to say some words that will set you free. Is that okay with you?"

He beeped once again.

"Okay, Percy. Rachel will say the words, and you will be free to be with Tallulah and Aubrey and Dot. Once you hear the words you will immediately go to them. You will not have to search for forgiveness anymore, for you have already been forgiven."

She nodded at me, and I stood up and read from a letter I'd found. It was a letter Aubrey had written while she still held out hope that Percy was alive.

"My love, I count the days until I see you again. Please come home to me soon. Come be with me. I cannot stand to think that I shall never again see your face. I would rather die a thousand deaths than do that. Please, my love, come to me." I put the paper on the table next to the lock of hair.

"Percy, you are free from this realm. You are no longer between two worlds because you have found forgiveness.

Those you wronged wait for you with love, not condemnation, on the other side. Go in confidence, Percy Ferguson, and may you finally enjoy the love you have always sought." The table and then the chairs began to shake. It was as if someone had turned up the power here, for the lights flickered high and finally blew out. Suddenly the window above the sink flung open and a whistling wind blew out of the house, out and up, up, up and away. And then Percy was gone. Gone to be with Aubrey.

We sat for a long time enjoying the peace his departure left behind. We'd done it together, and we'd done it safely. At some point, we might have to deal with Michael, but for now, we'd be okay.

Everyone would be okay.

Epilogue—Carrie Jo

The doorbell rang, but by the time I got there whoever wanted my attention had driven away. I stepped out on the porch, pulling the short robe tightly around me, and stared at the back of the Toyota as it pulled down the street. Hmm…no car I recognized. I waved at the neighbor who was conveniently digging in the flowerbed that she'd planted along our fence line. "Good morning!"

"Oh, good morning, Carrie Jo! Nice robe!" she said sarcastically.

Feeling equally sarcastic, I dipped a curtsy and walked back in the house. Yep, it was time to move. We were a growing family anyway, and having some extra space would be good for us all. What would Ashland think about country living? Maybe it was time to put some distance between us and downtown Mobile. It was definitely something to think about.

The guys were still asleep, so I pattered into my office, my slippers slapping on the wooden floor. I reached for the letter opener and sliced open the big manila envelope. I pulled the note card out first. It was a neatly written message from Detra Ann's detective friend, Brendan Bennett. He'd been integral to helping her get leads on Aleezabeth.

I think you'll find this interesting. Check your inbox tonight for more information. BB

And that was it. When Detra Ann said he was a man of few words, she wasn't kidding. "Okay, mister." I slid out the remaining papers. There were some newspaper clippings and photographs, and some of the pictures appeared to be fairly recent. My legs felt wobbly, and I plopped down in the seat. As I held the black and white photo in my hand I could hardly believe it. This was Chance. Although I could not remember him as a baby, I knew it was him! He had my eyes and was tall. He had a family of his own, a lovely wife and a good job as a teacher and...he was living in Pensacola, Florida!

The rush of information was too much for me. My own brother was only an hour away. I didn't know whether to laugh or cry, so I kind of did both.

"What's that?" Ashland asked quietly. He'd been so stand-offish lately, but that didn't matter now. I'd found my brother. I found Chance!

"Come see! A delivery driver just left it. It's from Brendan Bennett."

Rubbing the sleep out of his eyes, Ashland leaned across the desk and examined the photos. "You know, you couldn't deny him if you tried. You two really favor one another. Any word on your father?"

I frowned and shuffled through the papers. "No, I don't see anything, but Detective Bennett told me to check my inbox tonight, that he'd have some other stuff for me. I wonder what it will be."

"No telling. This is great news. I'm really happy for you. I'm going to whip up some omelets. You want one? Ham and cheese?"

I stared at him like he was crazy. I'd just found my brother, and he was acting like it was just another morning. "Um, no thanks. I think I'll stick with fruit today." The baby was awake now, judging by the "call of the wild one" coming from upstairs. Ashland didn't offer to bring him down, so I reshuffled the papers and went myself.

What was happening? I felt like I was on a train heading in one direction when I really needed to go the other way. So how did I stop the train?

I couldn't figure it out, but I wasn't going to worry about my husband's moodiness right now. I'd found my brother! I couldn't wait to see the look on my mother's face when I told her the good news.

At least she'd be happy for me. For us both.

Read more from M.L. Bullock

The Seven Sisters Series

Seven Sisters
Moonlight Falls on Seven Sisters
Shadows Stir at Seven Sisters
The Stars that Fell
The Stars We Walked Upon
The Sun Rises Over Seven Sisters

The Idlewood Series

The Ghosts of Idlewood
Dreams of Idlewood
The Whispering Saint (forthcoming)
The Haunted Child (forthcoming)
The Heart of Idlewood (forthcoming)

The Desert Queen Series

The Tale of Nefret
The Falcon Rises
The Kingdom of Nefertiti
The Song of the Bee-Eater (forthcoming)

The Sugar Hill Series

Wife of the Left Hand
Fire on the Ramparts (forthcoming)
Blood by Candlelight (forthcoming)
The Starlight Ball (forthcoming)
Athena's Revenge (forthcoming)

To receive updates on her latest releases,
visit her website at MLBullock.com
and subscribe to her mailing list.